THE LAW OF REVENGE

Choose your battles!

Abby

By the same author

Love you Forever

Abby is seventeen when he first falls in love. Shalini loves him too, and wants to marry him. But after three years of their relationship, she dumps him brutally one day, leaving him with a torturous set of unanswered questions.

He changes for the worse, and he is happy. But love shows up in his life again, this time in the form of Myra, who he marries. She changes him back to his innocent self, but when life throws a curve, she herself turns evil. Just when he gets things in control, Shalini makes a comeback.

Will he dump Myra and their son Rey for Shalini, or will Myra walk away with Rey?

THE LAW OF REVENGE

SECRETS NEVER DIE

ABBYSHEK CHANDRA

Srishti
PUBLISHERS & DISTRIBUTORS

Srishti Publishers & Distributors
A unit of AJR Publishing LLP
212A, Peacock Lane
Shahpur Jat, New Delhi – 110 049

editorial@srishtipublishers.com

First published in India by
Srishti Publishers & Distributors in 2024

10 9 8 7 6 5 4 3 2 1

Printed and bound in India

Dedicated to
The Universe

Acknowledgements

Without the following people, this book that you have in your hands would probably still be in the works.

You, my readers: I am hugely indebted and grateful to you for bestowing me with so much love for my debut novel, *Love You Forever*. Please keep it coming. It encouraged me to write *The Law of Revenge*. Thank you for believing in me and waiting patiently for my next.

Vagisha, my wife: Apart from being my best friend, she is my best critic who always shoots her unfiltered feedback at me from point-blank range. If it were not for her valuable inputs, this novel would have come out very differently from what it finally did.

Ryan, my elder son: The title of the novel, *The Law of Revenge* was suggested by Ryan and it fit beautifully with the story. He is always full of creative ideas and is my go-to person for unbiased suggestions in life.

Sean, my younger son: Sean is my never-ending source of entertainment and love. He keeps a tab on my heart rate and calms me down (when he thinks I am stressed) with his cute massages and stories.

Prof K.C. Sinha and Mrs. Indu Sinha, my parents: I am what I am because of their unconditional love, support, blessings and best wishes. They have always encouraged me to pursue my dreams.

Mrs. Laxmi Sinha and Mr. K. K. Verma, my parents-in-law: I know their blessings are always with me.

Jayanta Sir: A big thank you for your unwavering belief in me and also for creating a platform like Srishti that has given so many bestselling authors to the publishing world.

Arup Bose, Publisher: A great leader who has always been available for addressing my queries. Thanks Arup, I really appreciate all that you do.

Stuti, Chief editor: She is not just a great editor, but also a wonderful person. Thank you for making this novel a crisper version of itself and for being patient with my edits.

Inaya, Rhythm and Vivaan, my niece/nephews: Life would be incomplete without their cute chirping.

Last but not the least, extending my gratitude to the entire team at Srishti Publishers for their efforts in bringing this book to light.

CHAPTER 1

Location: Mumbai
Time: September 2019

"One Marlboro Lights please," I asked the roadside cigarette vendor, some hundred metres from my apartment.

It was 7 a.m. on a pleasant Sunday morning. I was done with my morning walk regimen around the streets of Lokhandwala and was headed home, but not before having my customary first cigarette of the day in open air. With this piece of slow poison and the morning fresh air, I often thought about my next move in life with a fresh mindset, especially with respect to nailing the politician's brother, Mahesh Prajapati – the son of a bitch who killed my wife, Myra.

"Today's cigarette is on me, sir," the vendor obliged.

"What's so special about today, your birthday?" I asked.

"No sir, just like that. Enjoy while it lasts." I failed to fathom his cryptic reply. Maybe, he was aware of what was going to happen and perhaps, also had a part to play in it.

Halfway back to my home from the cigarette vendor, I was intercepted by a white Mahindra Bolero with three men (two in the front and one in the rear) asking for directions to a nearby address. The two men in the front could not understand the directions I gave them. So, the third man (in the rear) intervened.

"Can you sit in the car and take us to the location?" he called me to the rear and opened the door for me to sit.

"I am afraid, I can't. I am getting late. Your destination is not too far from here. Just go straight ahead for about two hundred metres and ask someone for this address again," I tried to excuse myself out of the situation and turned away.

"Your name is Abby, right?" he asked.

"How do you know my name?" I turned back, startled.

Before I could wrap my head around what was going on, a fourth man from behind pushed me inside the car with the third one pulling me inside simultaneously. And in a matter of a few seconds, amidst the chirping of birds on a peaceful Sunday morning, I was abducted.

"What are you doing? Who the fuck are you?" I demanded as the two hefty, sweaty and stinky men on both sides held my hands tight behind my back and tied them up.

"Mumbai Police," the third guy flashed his ID in front of my face. His first name was hidden under his finger but from what was visible, his surname was Bhide.

As the car sped away, they put the 'Police' placard on the dashboard so that nobody would question them on their way to wherever they were taking me. There was no police beacon or light bar atop the car, making me doubt if they really were the police. And if they were, they were not using the official police car, which meant they were doing something beyond the confines of the law.

"But what have I done?" I asked as Bhide dug out my phone from my pocket and turned it off.

"You don't know what you have done? Are you really that foolish or you are pretending?" Bhide barked.

"Stop fooling around. You can't pick me without a warrant. Show me the warrant," I argued.

"Motherfucker, we can pick you without a warrant and do whatever the hell we want. You see this?" Bhide flashed his pistol in front of my face.

"This is my artificial dick that ejaculates bullets. Keep your bloody mouth shut now or this thing will cum inside your backside," Bhide warned.

I gulped the saliva down my dry throat as my heart started throbbing.

"Kulkarni, blindfold this idiot," Bhide ordered the fourth guy who was sitting on my other side.

"Listen, my son is very young and all alone at home. Can we please turn around and go to my home? He will look for me when he wakes up and if he doesn't find me, he will be scared. I need to inform him that I will be away for a while. I will also need to make arrangements for him. Please understand. I am sure you guys have kids too," I pleaded as Kulkarni blindfolded me.

"All alone? Really? So, you have kept that 24x7 maid (Simmi) only for your 'bang-bang'?" Bhide started laughing hysterically, with the rest of his men joining in.

"Don't act smart with us. Until you return home, if at all you do, Simmi will take care of your son," Bhide continued.

I wanted to rough Bhide up real bad. Only if god had somehow bestowed me with an 'artificial dick' like Bhide's, even if it was for a fleeting moment, I would have shown him and his accomplices its orgasmic powers for real.

"*Calm down, Abby. These guys seem to know a lot about you. One mistake from your side and you will only be able to repent for what they can do to Rey and to you,*" inner Abby talked.

"*What is the guarantee they won't do anything to Rey or me if I just play along? What if I repent not resisting this abduction?*" I debated inner Abby amidst the stress of an unprotected Rey back home with Simmi, who I now did not completely trust.

"*You want to resist four armed men, who are either cops or goons? Either way, not advisable. So, cut the crap and do what they say. We don't really have options at the moment,*" inner Abby tried to beat some sense into my mind.

"Sir, we have him. We are taking him to the site," Bhide called someone from his phone.

"Bhide sir, whatever the issue is, we can talk and sort it out. If you know what I mean, we can hammer out a deal," I threw my last and only card.

"Bugger, you want to bribe a cop? Let this get over. Then I will show you how to work out a deal," Bhide smacked me on the back of my head. So, they were actually cops who were goons.

"*You deserved it, Abby. Now keep your dim-witted mouth shut for some time and put your other senses to work,*" inner Abby mocked my blunder.

"*Bhide will have to pay for all this,*" I told inner Abby.

"*Save that thought for later. Your focus right now should be to get out of this situation unscathed,*" inner Abby prioritized.

In about twenty minutes, the car stopped somewhere and I was pushed into what seemed like an enclosed place, a room maybe. Figuring out why I was in such a situation was pretty simple. I had no animosity with anyone in the world, except Mahesh Prajapati. There was no doubt that all of this was done at his behest. My assumption was soon confirmed when he walked in an hour later.

"So Mr Abby, I hope these guys did not trouble you much. I am sorry if they did," Mahesh said as he removed my blindfold.

Like I had guessed, I was in a room, tied to a chair with Mahesh standing in front of me. At over six-foot height, he was a towering, muscular and fair-skinned man; someone who was too good-looking for his name and definitely cut out for a career in Bollywood.

His stooges were scattered around the room, along with Bhide and his team. With the time it took Bhide to get me to this location, it was most probably a bungalow or a house in Madh Island, but it mattered the least at that point in time.

"Why am I here, Mahesh?" I asked, desperately trying to free myself.

"You know the answer, Abby. Despite umpteen warnings to drop the case against me, you have been relentlessly pursuing it. It is pointless. You will not get anything out of it. It will be dismissed," he said, smirking at my helplessness.

"Why are you bothered then? Let it get dismissed. Why abduct me for it?" I replied.

"You know how the system works here, don't you? It is the system you trust that brought you here for me, almost illegally. You think it is going to bring justice to you? Not at all! Snap out of the ideal world that you create in your novels, Abby. Whatever has happened, has happened. Nothing you do can bring back your wife. However, anything you do may sabotage your present and your future," he threatened me.

"I still don't understand. Let's assume you run the system and it is not going to give me justice. Then let it be that way. Why are you behind my life to withdraw the case?

"I will tell you what I think. The cops might be working for you, but the judicial system doesn't. You are restless because the elections are around the corner and your politician brother wants a clean image of you (and him), bereft of any criminal charges. So, all you can do is, threaten me so that I withdraw the case and set you free. I smell nothing but helplessness in your words," my inherent combative nature discounted what inner Abby had advised me to do.

"Shut the fuck up! I can threaten you and also act on those threats. You are right; I have the cops in my pocket and that power is enough to bring you down to your knees. You are seeing the trailer of it, as we speak. I have been very 'lenient' until now, if I may use that word, but I cannot guarantee sticking to that approach, going forward. I had not imagined the issue would stretch for four years. It's high time we end it now," he pulled my hair bringing his face closer to mine.

"Also, to shake you out of your hallucination, I have bought out all your witnesses. The CCTV footage is also not available because the security cameras in the area were 'obviously' not operational at the time of the accident, thanks to my handsome payments to the concerned people. There is nothing left for you. All I want for me and you is a peaceful exit from this," he chucked my hair and walked away from me.

"Do whatever, but the case will still take time to close and till the time it is open, the other political outfits will continue to make an issue out of it, in their election campaign. I won't let you off the hook so easily," I tried to keep up my courage.

"Well then, it is your personal choice Abby and only you will be responsible for the dire consequences that await you."

"You can't kill me. You will be the prime suspect if you do," I rationalised with him.

"Yeah, I can't kill you. However, I can turn your life into such a hell that you will pray each day, to die. There are so many accidents happening every day, so many kidnappings happening too. Who else would know better than you? You have seen both the situations now. I am sure you would not want your son to meet with an accident or get kidnapped. I mean, I am just saying." Mahesh's words ran a chill down my spine.

"Don't bring my son into all of this."

"I'll have to do it. You've left me with no choice. Trust me, if you don't agree to withdraw the case, something terrible will happen and it could be to you, Rey, your parents, or anybody else you care about," he warned me.

"If anything happens to them, I will tear you into pieces, no matter what the consequences," I yelled at him.

"Why wait for all that to happen? Withdraw the case, as simple as that."

"I won't," I was adamant.

"For god's sake, what the hell is your problem? Who are you fighting for, your wife? Do you even know who your wife really was? Do you know what she was doing behind your back while you were busy slogging and selling your dream (Eduwiser) off to gift her that dream penthouse in Dubai?" he sounded very sure about his words.

"What do you mean?" I was rattled.

"She deserved to die. If anything, you should be thanking me for getting rid of her. Who knows, she purposely jumped in front of my car to commit suicide because she was ashamed of what had happened in her life?" he continued his rant, ignoring my question.

"Dare you talk about my Myra like that! I will rip your tongue out of your mouth," I roared in anger as I helplessly tried to free my hands and walk my talk to deprive him of his tongue.

"Oh yes, I will. The whole world will and you won't be able to do anything about it. Just in case you don't quit the case, the details of it (what I just enlightened you on) and more will make their way into the courtroom and also the media. I have proof to corroborate all what I have said and trust me, it's not pretty. This will be a bonus repercussion in addition to making you suffer. Myra is dead Abby, let her be in peace with your reputation and hers intact. Back out," he suggested.

Mahesh had stumped me. I had nothing to say except deal with the tears that came rushing into my bloodshot eyes.

"I understand you will take time to process what I have said and I will allow you that luxury. I will have you dropped at the place where you were picked up from in the morning. Take a couple of days, think it through and file the withdrawal of the case by this Wednesday. You are a good man, Abby. Go back and start a new life," he added.

"Bhide, drop him back," he ordered as he walked off.

CHAPTER 2
(RECAP OF LOVE YOU FOREVER)

Location: Patna - Mumbai - Dubai
Time: May 2000 - September 2016

Abby (son of a famous Mathematician in Bihar) was in Grade 12, when he fell in love with Shalini at an IIT Coaching Institute in Patna and their story mostly continued over secret phone calls. After their high school, Abby managed to get into IIT Roorkee while Shalini got into Rajgad Institute of Technology, Karnataka and their long-distance relationship began.

Abby loved Shalini a lot and considered her his goddess, but she took his love for granted and was perennially rude to him. Due to her disrespectful behaviour and frequent avoidance, he wasn't sure if she wanted to marry him. So, at the end of their second year in 2003, he decided to travel to Rajgad and ask her in person what she really wanted.

Shalini's affirmation to his marriage proposal put all his doubts to rest. But, barely a year later, in April 2004, she suddenly dumped him one day, saying that her marriage had been fixed to some other guy chosen by her parents. Despite repeated pleas, she refused to fight for him and told him to never get in touch with her. He moved on, completely broken and angry, assuming he'd never find out why she deserted him, completely ignorant that a decade later, she'd make a comeback to disrupt his life once more. During the placements in August 2004, he secured a job offer from L&T, Mumbai where he joined in after completing his graduation.

Later in the year 2006, during the course of his MBA applications, he came across Myra's profile on a social networking platform. He befriended her online for a casual fling, but she fell for him and his conscience forced him to give in. He convinced Myra's parents and his, and they agreed to their marriage, which could happen only after Myra's and Abby's elder siblings' marriages.

On the professional front, he made it to ISB Hyderabad for his MBA, which he joined in April 2007. During his MBA, Myra's mother pressurized him for court marriage, citing societal concerns. Considering it harmless, he agreed. The frequency of their visits to each other increased after that, each accompanied by an unbearable pain of parting.

During campus placements at ISB, Abby bagged a coveted job in Dubai. He left for Dubai in July 2008 while Myra stayed in Mumbai as they could not live together until they married publicly. Chasing his dreams of entrepreneurship, he soon quit his job and returned to India in December 2008, only to face severe resistance from everyone, but he persevered and stood his ground.

Driven by his versatility, his publishing venture (Eduwiser) set off to a flying start, but not without a simultaneous deterioration of his relationship with Myra. Their public marriage happened in December 2009 and amidst the excitement of living together after marriage, their relationship recovered.

Since family support was minimal, he took care of Myra when she got pregnant about two years later. In August 2012, their son (Rey) arrived and turned their lives upside down. Due to different styles of parenting and unfair distribution of household work, differences started creeping in their relationship, again. From an angel, Myra turned into a demon, placing unreasonable demands and subjecting Abby to domestic violence on a number of occasions. A depressed and friendless Abby became a chain-smoker to survive while Myra turned to her friends for emotional support.

Life continued on the same note until Abby's birthday in January 2015, when Shalini made a comeback, giving him an opportunity to ask why she had refused to fight for him. She told him that she had tried to discuss about him with her mother, but she threatened to commit suicide. So, she backed off completely. She further told him that a few months after their break-up, she got engaged to her current husband, while she was still in her final year. Abby's intuition about her having an affair with some other guy proved correct when she confessed to a relationship she had with her batchmate (Sunny) in her final year, two months after her engagement. Despite being engaged to her current husband, she had fought with her parents for him. As Karma would have it, Sunny disappeared on her, leaving her with no option but to marry her current husband. She said she still loved Abby and apologized for hurting him. Abby's decade old feeling of anger finally attained *moksha* and he forgave her to make her his good friend.

Abby recalled the ideal partner he was when he was in a relationship with Shalini, the type of partner he had always thought he would be to his wife. Realizing Myra was going through postpartum depression and that she needed his unconditional support and not his anger, he promised himself to change to the original Abby, the one who remained calm and kept his love as priority at all times.

He apologized to Myra for everything hurtful he had done and asked her to start over. Love made a powerful comeback in their lives, and he decided to sell off his dream (Eduwiser) to realize hers (him quitting entrepreneurship to take up a job and buying a penthouse in Dubai to shift to, for good), while she had no idea about this decision of his. On their court marriage anniversary in July 2015, she surprised him with the news of her second pregnancy.

Soon after, Abby's debut novel (based on their lives) got accepted by a leading publisher. The first printed copy of the novel was expected a few days before her birthday in October. Though Myra begged him to let her read the final draft of the novel, he declined her request saying she could read it when he would gift her the first printed copy of it. In August, Abby finally purchased a sprawling penthouse in Dubai, but kept Myra in the dark about it because he wanted it to be her surprise birthday gift. On her birthday, he had also thought of telling her about his plan to shift to Dubai for good because she always wanted to settle there.

Everything seemed perfect, but ten days before her birthday on 1st October, destiny decided to play a spoilsport. Abby was supposed to get the first printed copy of his novel directly from the printing press the next evening. Since Myra had her routine sonography scheduled at the same time, he postponed his plan and decided to accompany her for the same. Late that night, he started chatting with Shalini about his surprise plans for Myra. He kept deleting the chats simultaneously so that Myra wouldn't get to know about the surprises, in case she browsed through his chats. Out of nowhere, Myra woke up and caught him red-handed chatting with Shalini. She demanded to check his phone, but he refused. A heated exchange of words ensued in which she accused him of having an extramarital affair. He finally showed her the chat, most of which was already deleted, and tried to explain, but she was in no mood to budge from her assumption. Hurt and angered by her distrust, he left for the printing press the next day to get his novel, instead of accompanying her to the sonography clinic.

As fate would have it, Myra and Rey met with an accident right outside their building when they were going to the clinic. Abby rushed to the hospital, but it was a little too late. Myra and his unborn child had left the world, but Rey survived with injuries. Abby promised Rey that he would make the culprit (Mahesh Prajapati, brother of a noted politician) pay for his deed.

Rey soon recovered, but Abby started spiralling down into depression. Noticing his failing health and frequent emotional breakdowns, his parents forced him (and Rey) to shift to Patna with them. Keeping Rey's future in mind, Abby then shifted to

Dubai in 2016 to turn into a full-time author, so that he could work from home and take care of Rey.

A year into his post-Myra life, his heart was still full of regrets and 'what-ifs'. Had he accompanied Myra to the clinic despite their fight, she would have been alive. Nothing could be worse than not being by her side when she breathed her last. He had made all of her dreams come true, but she did not even get to know about them, leave aside living them. He had written the book for her, which had become a bestseller, but she never got to read it and it was only because he had not let her when he easily could have. Last but not the least, they had parted on a bitter note and he did not even get a chance to apologize to her.

He revisited Myra's blank email that she had sent minutes before her accident and through an unintentional fluke, recovered its hidden content. In the email, Myra had apologized for her rude behaviour and confessed that she came to know about the Dubai penthouse surprise while browsing through his inbox the night before the accident, when she was checking for any email exchange between Shalini and him. She also pleaded guilty to reading his novel on his laptop in June 2015 itself.

The email got rid of most of his regrets and he finally made peace with her death. The court case, however, was still going on in India and the accused, Mahesh, was out on bail.

CHAPTER 3

Location: Dubai
Time: October 2016 - July 2018

Though I was absolved by Myra in her last mail and it had helped me make peace with her death, the oasis of peace soon faded away like a mirage, with the unfinished business of getting Mahesh Prajapati to pay for his deed, still lingering in my mind. I could not let that loathsome toad get away with what he had done.

My fight was obviously legal and through the Indian judicial system that I had some faith in. I knew the process would be slow and frustrating, but I was ready for the long haul. Every time a hearing was scheduled, I flew down from Dubai to Mumbai a day before the assigned date while my mom flew from Patna to Dubai to be with Rey, a couple of days before I left for Mumbai. The process was burning a hole in my pocket, but I could not think of any other safer and cheaper option.

There were times when the hearing was scheduled and I reached the court on time, but the judge did not show up at all. At other times, the judge arrived late and before my case's turn came, the court's time ended and the hearing got postponed to the next date that was a month or two later.

Quite a few times when the judge was present, Mahesh's lawyer skipped the hearing and we got a new date. A lot of my money was going down the drain, but I kept at it because if the law ultimately punished Mahesh, all the money 'wasted' would be money 'utilized'.

At times when I got lucky and the hearing did happen, routine questions were asked repeatedly and that too, only from me. Details like the relationship between me and Myra, the exact dates and the times when different events happened, Myra's life insurance policy, names of my family members and what they did for a living, etc., were asked, confirmed and reconfirmed in subsequent hearings. I was supposed to memorize all the details like a tenth grader in India. Slight mistake in the time or the date of any event and there would be a barrage of irrelevant questions fired at me with the court getting adjourned after that. For some unknown reason, the accused was never called to the dock for questioning, except once when he was granted bail and it seemed more like I was the accused. Fighting a case in India required godly patience which I often used to run out of.

It wasn't that Mahesh was a mute bystander who was not taking any steps to get off the hook. I used to get abusive and threatening WhatsApp calls from multiple numbers asking me to withdraw the case. After I received a few such calls, I stopped picking calls from unknown numbers and it did serve as a big relief. Nothing eventful happened as no threat issued to me was ever executed. I could not take legal action against Mahesh for such calls because there was no concrete proof of his connection to them and I did not want to file a series of formal complaints against unknown callers. The current case's legal process was consuming enough for me and I did not want to digress either. Honestly, I could also not afford to fight against tens of others simultaneously.

Workwise, I had already quit entrepreneurship and my corporate life, and was a full-time author based out of Dubai; after my debut novel turned into a national bestseller. However, my next novel would take time. I was barely writing anything because I was not in that mind frame to think about and write a compelling story due to all that was happening in my life. That I had to single-handedly take care of Rey, made things tougher.

When things look dark, there's always a silver lining. For me, that silver lining was Shalini. From the time Myra left the world, she was constantly by my side, though via calls and messages, and had proved herself to be an epitome of true friendship, just like she had promised. She was someone I could have uninhibited conversations with, without being judged, and I really needed that. Even the strongest of people in the world need someone to confide in and I was no exception.

It all restarted with Shalini's tens of calls the very next day after Myra's demise and I had picked none of them because I did not want to talk to anyone. I had no idea how she got to know about Myra because I don't think anyone had put that up on social media that soon. Her missed calls were followed by a WhatsApp message.

"Hi Abby, are you ok? Just heard about Myra. I am so, so sorry for your loss. I know how much you loved her. I can understand you not feeling like talking to anyone right now and I respect that. If you need anything, know that I am just a call or a message away; please don't hesitate. I will drop everything and come down to Mumbai right away if you need me by your side."

"Thanks for being there, Shalini. Will call back," I had replied a day later.

"I know you always prefer fighting your battles alone and don't need anyone's support, but I am worried for you. Please do call back whenever you can," she had messaged.

I remember calling her when I shifted to Patna (from Mumbai) in January 2016, about three months after Myra had left the world. What started with a message and then my first call to her post Myra, turned into daily calls by the time I shifted to Dubai.

Rey was totally on me with four hours of school every day followed by a couple of hours of creche time, allowing me some 'me-time' to maintain my sanity. I often used this time to talk to Shalini, because it was the time that also suited her the most. She used to be in her office that time, away from her orthodox husband's prying eyes and her daughter - Sia, who was just two months older than Rey.

There was nothing romantic about our calls. I don't think either of us was inclined romantically towards the other. From her side, the conversations were daily updates on what happened at office and at home, how Sia was doing and what the plan was for the upcoming days.

From my side, it was more or less a similar update sprinkled with my frustration about the ongoing court case. The interactions with her were helpful, especially with respect to Rey. From what Rey ate to how much he slept, what he studied, how many days he missed school, who his friends were, what he liked/disliked, etc., she knew almost every detail and always had them at her finger-tips. In the absence of Myra, she virtually took care of him and probably knew more about him than I did, as his 'pseudo' mother. I often wondered how she did it all, in addition to managing her own house, office and Sia. I would be lying if I said I wasn't touched by her care and attention.

From what I had heard from her about her husband Prashant, he was a male chauvinist and belonged more to the previous generation who believed men were superior to women. He was of the view that the kid(s) along with all the household work, including paying all the bills, school fees, etc., was the sole responsibility of the wife and he was privileged as a man to be free of such duties so that he could focus only on his work and himself. As a husband, his only duties were to lend his surname and sperm to his wife, in addition to a house that he had bought in his name.

That he didn't love Shalini was pretty evident from the incidents she told me about. Even when a husband does not love his wife, chances are he would still love his daughter - his own blood. But even that wasn't the case with Prashant and I came to know about it when Shalini called me one day in the evening, an odd time for our call.

"Hey, how are you?" she asked.

"I am fine. An unusual time for our call. All good?" I asked.

"Yeah. What are you doing?"

"I was watching YouTube videos with Rey."

"Not more than half an hour of videos for him, ok?" she said in a voice that did not seem free-flowing.

"Shalini, are you crying?" I signalled Rey to continue watching the videos on his iPad and excuse me for the call.

"No, I am not. I am having cold it seems," she tried to control her outburst.

"Come on Shalini, I know you enough to smell something wrong. Tell me what happened," I insisted.

"A nasty fight with Prashant. I was stuck at work for an important meeting. I had requested Prashant to leave work early today so that he could pick Sia from the creche by the 6 p.m. deadline, which he did grudgingly. I left office by 6 and was expected to reach home by 7. All he had to do was take care of Sia until then. When I reached home at around 7, I saw him dangling Sia out of the balcony, threatening to fling her if she did not stop bawling," she managed to speak in between her intermittent gasps for breath.

"That idiot did not understand that his daughter might have been cranky because she was hungry or tired," she continued.

"Well, even if he did not understand the reason, holding her the way he was is not justified," I replied because his act had enraged me, though I did not want to say anything against Prashant that would widen the rift between a wife and her husband.

"Exactly! Tell me Abby, what if she had slipped by mistake? Doesn't he have a heart of a father? Isn't Sia his daughter too? What kind of a father does this? You are also a father. Would you do this to Rey?" she was crying inconsolably.

"Never, but I guess everyone is different. Maybe he is pushed to the wall due to work-related stress and it got vented out on Sia. I am sure, what he did was just to scare her. Talk it out with him," I tried to bridge the gap.

"Done with him now. I am just waiting for the divorce to go through," she blurted in anger.

"Divorce? What are you talking about?" I was taken aback.

"Yes...uh, I am sorry. I should have told you before, but you have been going through a lot yourself and I would be the last person to add to your stress," she reasoned.

"Shalini, it's been more than two years since the tragedy."

"I know, but I don't think you are over it yet, Abby."

"Oh, come on! That is not an acceptable reason."

"I said I am sorry. I agree, I should have told you before."

"I don't understand. Why divorce? Are things so bad between the two of you?"

"Things are not bad between us; they are the worst they can be between a husband and a wife."

"However bad things are, they can always be sorted out through dialogue. You guys are acting in haste. Meet a marriage counsellor, discuss and set boundaries for each other in your relationship, do whatever but don't opt for divorce. It is never the solution, especially when you have a daughter involved. Imagine what Sia would have to go through."

"She will have a better life without him. She also hates him as much as I do, if not more."

"It is not about that Shalini. I don't know. Maybe, I shouldn't interfere in your personal matters. I suggested what I felt was right. It is your life and you have the right to take your decisions."

"See, this is how an ideal husband should be. When a woman marries a man, she doesn't become his slave. She has her own life and should have the right to decide for herself. For me, Prashant decides where I work, what time I return from office, what car we will buy, which house we will buy, etc. And then, I am left to execute his decisions," she was clearly upset.

"I am not an ideal husband, Shalini! If I were, Myra would be alive. Anyway, let's cut it. Your parents are fine with the divorce?" I asked her.

"They are with me on it. It is a simple thing, Abby. Just because I took the wrong decision of marrying the wrong guy, it doesn't mean I should stick to it for my entire life, trying to make that wrong guy the right one. I would be a fool to continue with such a marriage even after realizing the blunder I did and knowing that my life will always be miserable with him."

"I take that point. I thought I was the only one fighting a court case. Now, we will identify even more with each other."

"The custody of Sia will be another battle if he decides to fight for it, just to harass me."

"I know, but think about it later. No point worrying about it right now."

"Right, there are still a few months for the divorce to go through, if there are no hiccups on the way."

"Yeah, so take things one at a time."

"Thanks Abby, I am feeling much lighter after talking to you. Listen, Prashant had gone down for a smoke and might be back any moment. Will call you tomorrow from office, ok?"

"Yeah, no problem. Take care."

"You too."

CHAPTER 4

Location: Dubai
Time: August 2018 - September 2018

By the time Rey turned six in August 2018, he had probably figured out that I was giving him false assurances of his mother returning post her long vacation. I knew that sooner or later, I would have to answer his inevitable and tough questions, and I didn't have to wait too long for it.

"Daddy, what does 'died' mean?" he asked one night when I was putting him to sleep.

"Where did you pick that word from?" I countered.

"Tell na," he insisted.

"I want to know who used that word," I demanded.

"My friend, Rachel. She told me her parents were talking that my mumma died."

"Oh, my baby!" I hugged him as tears showed up in my eyes.

His teacher knew about Myra and the news must have reached Rachel's parents directly or indirectly. Though it irked me, the positive side of it was that it opened a window of opportunity for me to tell him about the harsh reality that both of us had to live with.

"Now can you tell me the meaning? Does it mean going on a long vacation?" he asked.

His questions put me at a loss of words. It took me a while to gather my thoughts and answer with the most suitable words, to have minimal impact on him.

"You know the world is primarily made of two types of things – living and non-living. Remember in school, they taught you about them and the differences between them?" I started explaining him.

"Yeah, living things are like us, the animals and the plants. Non-living things are like my toys," he was quick with the answer.

"Correct. Now, every living thing has a life cycle. It is born as a baby, then the baby grows into a child, the child grows into an adult, the adult then grows old and finally, leaves the world. This cycle of life is called the life cycle of an individual. When it ends, he leaves the world and we say that he died. Every living thing has to go through the end stage of dying because one day, his life cycle has to come to an end.

"Mumma's life cycle also ended, though a little early. So yeah, Mumma died," I tried to clear my throat that was choked with grief.

"It is the law of nature and a normal thing. My life cycle will also end one day and so will everyone else's, whoever is around in this world. Not a big deal," I tried to trivialize death with my emotionally loaded voice.

"People who die, do they ever come back?" he asked.

"Unfortunately, no."

"So, I will never be able to meet my mumma?" I sensed his voice becoming softer.

"No, but you can see her," I tried to manoeuvre him away

from despair.

"What? Where?" he was surprised.

"In the sky. Many people believe that people turn into stars after their life cycle ends. So, your mother is a star now and she is watching over you from up there to protect you from all things evil."

"I want to see her," he jumped off the bed and ran towards the terrace.

"Right now?"

"Yeah! Come na, Daddy," he had a smile on his face, to which I couldn't say no.

"Ok, coming," I followed.

"There are so many stars. Which one is Mumma?"

"That star, the brightest one. She is your mother."

"Wow! Beautiful. I will talk to her daily now."

"As you wish."

"Daddy, she died because of that car accident?" he asked as we returned to our bed.

"Yes, baby."

"Punish the driver, Daddy. Give him a harsh punishment. He sent Mumma so far away from me."

"I promise, I will," the fire of revenge in me that had started flickering with time burst into flames.

The legal battle was moving at snail's pace, if at all it was and I could not just be a sitting duck, waiting for things to happen on their own. I had to think of something to expedite the delivery of justice.

"*It's taking forever for the case to move towards closure. What do I do?*" I asked inner Abby that night.

"*That is how things work in India, at least. You can't do much about it,*" inner Abby replied.

"But isn't justice delayed justice denied?" I asked.

"Not the correct question. The correct questions are whether or not we can trust our judicial system to deliver justice at all and what is our Plan B if Plan A (delivery of justice through the legal system) is headed towards failure?" inner Abby responded.

"I feel we can trust our system. Though justice might be delayed, the accused will surely be punished."

"You are naïve, Abby. Anyways, be happy with your belief. I don't have faith in our system."

"What is Plan B then?"

"Take control of the situation and deliver justice yourself. Now is the age of D2C (Direct to Consumer) services."

"Are you nuts? I am not going against the law. Besides that, I am not powerful enough to harm Mahesh in any way."

"The real power lies in the head Abby, and I know you are more powerful than Mahesh that way. Trust yourself."

"Tell me what to do next."

"I am not sure if staying in Dubai is helping your case. You should contemplate moving back to India. Who knows, Plan A might get fast-tracked and there is no need for Plan B. If there is a need for it, we will think about it that time."

"I agree, it is definitely a point worth mulling over, but shifting to India is a big decision and involves Rey. I don't want to rush my decision and expose him to any kind of risk (due to Mahesh). Let's give the idea some time to settle in my head."

The seeds of 'moving back to India' had been planted in my head. All they needed was some water to germinate and that water was provided by my best friend, Shalini when I met her for the first time after our break-up more than fourteen years ago.

CHAPTER 5

Location: Dubai - Patna
Time: October 2018 - November 2018

Shalini's divorce came through in October and she was beatific when it happened.

"Abby, I got the divorce! Yippie!" she called me from the court itself and I could sense the relief in her voice.

"Hey, congratulations! Finally!" I was happy for her.

"Thank you."

"Where are you?" I asked.

"Still at the family court. I just wanted to share the good news with you. I will call you later to speak at length. Cool?"

"Yeah, sure. Take your time."

"Hey, now tell me," she called me later at night.

"You tell me. How does it feel?" I asked.

"It feels like a huge burden on my head has been lifted. I feel liberated and free."

"Happy 'Independence Day'," I smiled.

"It is indeed my Independence Day," she laughed.

"What about Sia?"

"I have her custody, but Prashant can visit her with prior intimation."

"Wow! How did he agree to it so easily?" I was surprised.

"I let go of the alimony and he agreed. As it is, Sia was a burden for him."

"And Sia is fine with this arrangement?"

"She is more than fine with it. She is happy."

"And what about the apartment? I think it was in Prashant's name," I was eager to know all the details.

"Dad is buying that apartment from him and Prashant is ok with it, as long as he gets his money. He will move out."

"Why not buy a new apartment?"

"That house has Sia's memories. I want it."

"I can understand. It might sound ironic but this calls for a party," I said to her, cheering her.

"Wherever and whenever you say, but for that, we will have to meet, right? When are you coming to India next?" she asked.

"The next hearing is scheduled for the last week of this month, just before Diwali. So, I will be in Mumbai that time."

"Ok, I will be in Patna that time for Diwali. Tanisha (Shalini's sister) and her husband are also visiting Patna (from the US) at the same time."

"Umm...In that case, I don't think we will be able to meet this time. Let's catch up next time for sure."

"Just a thought, why don't you come to Patna for Diwali, after the hearing?" she asked me.

"Patna? I mean, I can, but I don't know. I haven't thought about it," I was startled at her offer.

"Then think about it. Call your siblings and their families to Patna as well. Rey will have a lot of fun with so many family members around. Aunty and uncle will obviously be very happy."

"That's there. Let me see."

"What see? When was the last time you were in Patna with your entire family, celebrating any festival?" she was persistent.

"I don't want to remember that time. Things were different then; my lifeline was there with me. Now, she is not."

"I am sorry, I didn't mean to make you sad."

"That's ok."

"Come na, Abby. It will be so exciting to be in Patna with you after so many years."

"Even if I come to Patna, how will we meet? I am sure your parents will not be open to that idea. So, what's the point?" I asked her.

"I know, but at least we will be in 'our' city, barely two kilometres apart from each other. Nostalgia is already getting me excited."

"You women get excited for weird reasons. Give me some time. Let me talk to Rey, Mom and my brothers before I confirm."

"You men will never understand. Plan this trip and you can thank me later."

"Let's see."

I would be wrong if I said I felt nothing at the thought of being in Patna at the same time as Shalini. There was definitely a tinge of that teenage excitement, that typical boyfriend-girlfriend feeling. Our relationship in Patna was very short-lived because soon after the proposal, both of us had moved to our respective colleges. And for the few months we were in Patna after the proposal, we were too strictly monitored by our respective parents to meet, apart from being occupied with our entrance examinations.

This time, it was going to be different. Our friendship was on another level, we were more than a decade older with kids and most importantly, we were equipped with the new age technology of 'private and exclusive' connectivity through our personal smartphones loaded with WhatsApp, Snapchat, Telegram, Instagram, Facebook, etc. All of this minus the pressure of life-changing examinations like JEE and Class 12 Boards, it was indubitably a scenario worth experiencing amidst the monotony of a stressful and grieving life.

When I proposed the idea to Mom, she was ecstatic and so was Dad. Both my brothers and their families were on board with the idea too. Rey was always up for travel to anywhere in the world, with Patna being his favourite destination because of the princely treatment meted out to him there. So, the Patna plan was on!

We landed in Patna on the last day of October, after the hearing in which nothing eventful happened. Our entire family had got together after a long time and there was festive mood at home. Mom had also invited a couple of her siblings with their families, which added to the happy atmosphere around.

Myra would have absolutely loved the family reunion. She was a complete people's person and would have filled our home and everyone's heart with positive vibrations of her loud laughter. If she were alive, she would have wanted Rey to get a whiff of this family time and of our culture. All thanks to Shalini, I was glad we decided to have this get-together.

"Hey, how was the flight?" Shalini messaged on WhatsApp.

"It was good," I replied.

"Such a bad idea to come to Patna, no?" she asked sarcastically.

"Thank you Shalini, Rey is loving it. There is a perennial smile on my parents' faces. Everyone here is happy."

"And you?"

"I have not thought about it."

"Abby, can I tell you something?"

"Yeah, please."

"Don't take me wrong. I understand your love for Myra. But don't let yourself get so consumed by it that it starts affecting people around you, especially Rey. It is your right to grieve and be in your own world all the time, but it is Rey's right to have his father with him, mentally and physically, at least sometimes. It is your parents' right to see their son smile genuinely for once. You are dealing only with Myra's loss but they are dealing with losing both, Myra and you. They don't deserve this, Abby. Rey doesn't deserve this. You are an idol for him. With your behaviour, you are unknowingly shaping him up to be an emotionally weak man. If Myra was there, she wouldn't want that."

"If I knew you were going to talk about this, I would have ended our conversation right then. It is easy to preach when you are out of your shit, Shalini. I hope life never slides your feet into my shoes to make you understand how it feels. Anyway, let's talk later," I turned off my phone without waiting for her reply.

I wasn't prepared for what Shalini had said and I reacted accordingly. I felt she was asking me to forget Myra and that triggered me off. It took me a day of constant mulling over and looking at Mom, Dad and Rey with half-hearted smiles for her points to make sense. I was actually being self-centered and thinking only about my feelings. What followed this realization was the regret of replying rudely to her when her intention was solely to help me see what I was blind to, my vision clouded with selfishness.

I could not call her directly because she could be around relatives who might ask her uncomfortable and intruding questions about me. So, I messaged her.

"Shalini, I am sorry. I should not have been rude. My bad," she read my message but did not respond.

"What you said makes sense. I am sorry, it took me a while to get my head around it. When you said it, it was very abrupt and it caught me unawares. I was not expecting it. However, that does not justify my rudeness. Hence, the apology," I messaged again after a few minutes.

I waited for her reply the entire day, but all I received was disappointment. Clueless as to what to do, I turned to the inner Abby.

"*I know it is my fault and I apologized, but I am not that old Abby anymore who would beg for her forgiveness,*" I told inner Abby.

"*Correct. You have already owned your mistake and apologized,*" inner Abby responded.

"*Now, I won't respond when she messages. I will block her,*" I said.

"*I don't think you mean that. You can't block her. You know what she said, has some meat in it and it was your fault to overreact without thinking. So, you can't be angry with her. Like you needed time to understand her point, maybe she needs some time too, to accept your apology. Allow her that time. Or, do something that entices her to reply,"* inner Abby knew my empty threat.

"*Something that entices her to reply? Like what?*" I asked.

"*You are an author. You will work out something,*" inner Abby challenged the author in me.

"*I 'was' an author,*" I mocked myself.

"*Once an author, always an author. Hackneyed but true,*" inner Abby signed off.

The next morning, I pinged Shalini on WhatsApp and unsurprisingly, did not get a reply. It was time to tempt her. When Rey was sorted with the family members for the next couple of hours, I borrowed Dad's car and left for her house, though I just knew its vicinity, not its exact location.

It took me less than ten minutes to reach there. While figuring out which house was hers among half a dozen independent houses in her lane, I messaged her.

"I am in front of your house. You want to reveal yourself?"

"What? Where are you? I can't see anyone in front of our gate," pat came her reply and I patted my back. I still had my mojo intact.

"Wait, which one is your house?" I asked.

"The only blue one in our lane."

"Found it. I am in a pearl white Tata Safari," I replied.

"I can see the car but not you," she messaged.

"Where exactly are you spying on me from? Show yourself from somewhere and at least say 'hi'," I messaged back.

"I can't. Dad is at home and I am leaving with him for my dentist's appointment. Why didn't you inform me earlier that you were coming?"

"Oh! You weren't responding. How would I have informed?"

"We are leaving in five minutes."

"Cool, I will wait here in the car."

"Are you crazy? Dad will recognize you," she was quick to reply.

"Enjoy the thrill you missed years ago. I am waiting."

"Stubborn!" her voice had a hint of elation.

"Don't worry, I will just be a mute spectator to your departure."

Minutes later, I saw her, the girl I was crazy for eons ago and she was just as beautiful as before, if not more. She was in her trademark jeans and kurta. She had obviously put on some weight but if anything, it added more to her charm. As she walked towards the gate to open it for her father to drive out the car, our eyes locked for a brief moment followed by her faint, mischievous smile and a surreptitious wave of her hand to signal 'hi'.

Staying true to my awkward ways, I did not know how to react. So, I did not even smile back at her. Her father didn't notice me and they left for the dentist's while I returned home.

There was an inexplicable, joyous feeling within me. I was in denial about it, but when your soul is genuinely happy, it shows on your face and in your behaviour, no matter how hard you try to dismiss it. People at home were quick to notice the change and comment.

"You had gone to meet someone?" Mom asked.

"Yeah, an old friend," I tried to keep things casual.

"Nice. Convey my 'thanks' to that friend," Mom said.

"Why?" I asked, looking at Mom.

"Because since the time you have come back, the perennial frown on your face has been replaced by a constant smile," moms know their children more than the children know themselves.

"Smile? I am not smiling," I persisted with my denial mode.

"See, even as you say this, you are smiling. Ask anyone in the house. But whatever it is, I am very happy. I, at least, got a glimpse of my old Abby. Otherwise, I had thought I would perish without ever seeing you genuinely smile for once," Mom got emotional.

"Ma, don't cry now. Your old, fun-loving Abby will be back. It will take some time, but he will be back, I promise," I pacified her, making the same promise to myself.

It was then that I decided that the remaining couple of days I was in Patna for, I would use Shalini as a pleasant diversion from my messed-up life. I felt, my family and I deserved that break.

Shalini and I chatted later at night, with her reliving the minuscule moment we had shared earlier that day and the elation it brought, and me thanking her for making Mom happy (though indirectly).

The next day, she called me after the rest of her family had left for some family lunch. She did not join them because she had an important office call.

"Hey, what's up?" I answered her call and scurried into my room to evade my family's prying eyes that were hunting for some gossip.

"Just done with my office call. I am not sure what I will do after talking to you. I am getting bored," she replied nonchalantly.

"Bored? Should I come there to entertain you?" I made a frivolous suggestion.

"Are you serious?"

"No, I was just kidding. It is too much of a risk to come to your house and meet you. Your family would be home any moment now because it is already well past lunch time. I don't want to be caught inside my ex's house with her, by her entire family. It will be very embarrassing. It is the stuff of nightmares," I noticed myself laugh.

"If you are not coming, don't joke about it. You just inflated my expectation and popped it the very next moment. You know I still like you," she avoided using 'love' in place of 'like'.

"Sorry, but I can actually dare to come down to your house," I started toying with the idea of living my nightmare.

"I don't understand when you are serious and when you are not," she sounded annoyed.

"Call Tanisha and ask her the ETA."

"Give me two minutes. I will call you back," she complied.

"They will leave in ten minutes and will take about half an hour to reach here," she confirmed.

"Enough for us to meet. I will get ready and leave in five minutes. I will need another ten minutes to reach your place. We will keep ten minutes as margin of safety. So, we will have roughly fifteen minutes to catch up," I wasn't sure about Shalini, but I signed up just for the thrill of it.

Since I didn't have the luxury of time to decide what to wear, I went ahead with my safest bet - white linen shirt and blue jeans atop red sneakers. Bathed in perfume, as I was about to leave, my maternal uncle cut in.

"Hey, where are you rushing to, all decked up?" he teased.

"You should never interrupt when someone is going out," Mom interjected before I could satiate his appetite for the details.

"*Beta*, you go," she added as if she knew I was going to meet the same friend who had brought a hint of a smile to my face, and she would do anything to protect it.

Shalini and I were on call when I reached her home, that was a two-storied independent building with a small garden and a couple of parking spaces on the cemented passage that led to the house from the main gate. She asked me to enter the main gate, walk straight ahead without looking around too much and turn right at the end of the cemented passage, towards the main door. I followed her instructions, walking confidently as if I owned the house and was familiar with every corner of it.

As I approached the main door, I saw her standing behind the collapsible iron grills that protected the main door, with a heavy 'Godrej' lock in her hand that she had just opened to let me in.

She looked elegant in a light green cotton salwar suit with her hair tied in a ponytail, her brown eyes accentuating her beauty. We just exchanged smiles; no hug, not even a handshake, only smiles and that was in line with our current relationship status of 'pure friendship'.

After letting me in, she quickly locked the grill back and latched the main door, and asked me to follow her upstairs to the first floor. I could feel the positive vibes of her home. It seemed as if it had always been waiting for me and was happy that I had finally arrived. We entered the living room and made ourselves comfortable on the sofa, sitting on opposite sides of the centre table.

"What will you have?" she asked.

"We barely have fifteen minutes with us. Let's not waste them in stuffing our bellies. We can sit and talk," I refused.

"I just called Tanisha and she said they are slightly delayed. They are going to leave in five minutes. So now, we have about twenty-five minutes plus the buffer of ten minutes," she smiled.

"That's some relief. You have Thums Up?" I opened my greedy mouth.

"I knew it! So, I ordered," she went into the kitchen and was back in a minute.

"I can't believe we are sitting together in my house. My heart is throbbing!" she exclaimed with a sparkle in her eyes.

I noticed she had no make-up on, but her face still glowed. As she talked, the inner Abby had to try very hard to keep the outer one from being drawn into her mesmerizing beauty. The longer I looked into her hypnotic eyes, the stronger they captivated me and I literally had to shake myself out of her spell every other minute. She could make out every time I got lost in her charm. In response, she blushed and smiled.

To distract myself, I started looking around the living room until my eyes crossed a familiar showpiece kept in an impeccable condition on one of the shelves. It was a musical, battery-operated, revolving dancing couple enclosed in a glass dome full of water and sparkles.

"Is that...?" I had just started my question.

"Yes, that's the first Valentine's Day gift you had sent me. We were in the first year at our respective colleges that time," she cut in with her answer and got up to hand it over to me.

"It still works," she continued and turned it on to prove her claim.

"You have still kept it?" I was stunned.

"It is special to me, as are the other gifts you gave me," she sank into her sofa again.

I was touched. Someone has to be truly in love to preserve your gift in such an unblemished, working condition even after sixteen years; that's a very, very long time for a five hundred-rupee glass showpiece.

"Can I give you a hug?" I was so overwhelmed with emotions that I could not help asking her.

"Yes," she replied unlike the old, insensitive and reserved Shalini.

I stood up and held out my hand to help her get up from the sofa.

"Chivalrous, as always," she clutched my hand.

As we hugged, I felt her stiff body soften in my arms as if the hug had relaxed her and her deep breaths corroborated my conclusion.

We held each other in a tight embrace, neither of us willing to let go. I wanted to cry out loud in her arms and vent out all the bottled-up anger, frustration and sorrow in my life. But I exercised restraint over myself in the name of being strong.

"Hey, are you ok?" she asked as I inadvertently tightened my grip on her.

I guess she understood what was going on in my head. She moved her face a little away from mine to check if there were tears in my eyes while I held her tightly around her waist. The moment our eyes locked into each other and she noticed tears in my eyes, she planted a gentle kiss on my lips. The unadulterated, familiar fragrance of her breath was still as intoxicating as it was years ago and I could not stop myself from kissing her back as her soft and warm lips quivered between mine.

Amidst the rebirth of our old emotions, we forgot we were on borrowed time. In fact, we overshot our buffer time as well and were playing with danger now. Imagine her family arriving right then and me having to face it or hide somewhere in the house with a humongous probability of getting caught. Thrilling but hugely embarrassing and avoidable.

The prolonged second kiss had left us both a little flustered, our hearts fluttering wildly, ready to jump out of our bodies any moment and jog away, taking our lives with them. I left my half-finished drink and took her leave, but not before another quick and trembling hug, and a peck on her lips. She came to drop me at the main door and bid me goodbye with a very big smile on her face.

"Throw away my drink and spray some perfume in the living room just in case my perfume's fragrance is still lingering in there. Don't leave any proof," I cautioned.

"Don't worry. I will take care of it," she replied calmly, like a pro.

I had an extremely narrow escape because her family returned within minutes of my departure. Nobody asked me anything when I returned home and I took off from where I had left, except that my pulse was still not ready to return to normal. It would obviously take some time. Nobody in the world, including me and Shalini, could have ever imagined what had happened where it happened. Life is truly unpredictable and has its own way of throwing unimaginable surprises, both good and bad.

We got on a call late that night when everyone else had slept.

"I hope nobody questioned you about any visitor?" I asked.

"Nobody, though they came home within minutes of you leaving," she replied.

"Close shave! Were you able to throw my drink and wash at least one of the glasses before they arrived?"

"I did not throw your drink."

"As in?"

"It was 'your' leftover drink and I wanted to taste it. So, I drank it."

"What? Why?"

"Just like that," she replied.

"I don't know what to say."

"I loved your fragrance," she manoeuvred the topic only to lead to something more blushful.

"Thanks, I was wearing a Chanel."

"The perfume was good but I was actually talking about your fragrance."

"Mine? My perspiration?"

"Not the perspiration either. Each body has a distinct smell of its own. I am talking about your distinct smell. I loved it."

"I had bathed in perfume. How did you manage to smell me?"

"From the nape of your neck, when we hugged."

"You are making me feel violated," I was embarrassed but somewhere, it felt good because it was Shalini who had broken into my extremely intimate space.

"You are cute," she burst into laughter.

"By the way, you look much more handsome in person than on social media," she complimented to steer the topic away.

"And you look beautiful everywhere," I complimented back.

"Aww...thank you. I am still to come to terms with what happened today. It was inarguably one of the most thrilling and incredible experiences of my life. Thank you for that too."

"In hindsight, I wonder why I took my chances. It could have turned ugly."

"Well, it turned out to be beautiful, at least for me."

That day was a welcome detour from my routine life, away from the constant stress I was living with and I was thankful for it. For the entire moment that I was with Shalini, not once did I think about anybody else. She had indeed served as a balmy distraction for me and I wished I were in India so that I could meet her more often, given that she lived in Pune and I would have lived in Mumbai, both cities very close to each other geographically.

Even after our intimate moment was over, there was no such awkwardness between us that we couldn't look each other in the eye for the remainder of our lives. There was an enigmatic level of comfort – both mental and physical, despite meeting after so long. Could she be the perfect antidote to my poisoned soul? Well, only time would tell.

CHAPTER 6

Location: Dubai - Mumbai - Pune
Time: November 2018 - June 2019

The exhilaration due to the couple of encounters with Shalini in Patna was short-lived and the hurricane of extreme guilt soon slammed into me when I reached Dubai. I felt as if I had cheated on Myra and forgotten about her to feed my unwanted vice. My vengefulness that had erupted into a blistering fireball within me when Rey had asked me to punish Mahesh Prajapati, seemed to have been doused by those moments with Shalini and the remorse was shredding me into pieces.

"*I had a moment of weakness with Shalini and I just could not hold myself in. I feel disgusted with myself. Did I cheat on Myra?*" I asked inner Abby.

"*You had a pleasurable escapade with your ex and during that time, you forgot about Myra, though briefly. I would not call that cheating because technically speaking, Myra and you are no longer together. Don't overthink. You have been through a lot and you deserved those moments with Shalini. Such things happen in the heat of the moment and if anything, it will only sharpen your focus on the revenge with renewed vitality. Having said that, if you get carried away due to Shalini or anyone else and let go of the culprit, that would be called cheating on Myra. You owe it to her to avenge her death,*" inner Abby helped wash off my penitence.

Just when the legal wheels actually began to grind during the next hearing in December, my lawyer threw a spanner in the works by being undercooked for the hearing, much to my annoyance. With him charging fees on per hearing basis, it was more in his interest to stretch the case to maximize his earnings than to bring it to climax. The silver lining to this was that it reopened the topic of me returning to India.

"*Had I been staying here in Mumbai instead of Dubai, I would have pushed the lawyer and taken updates from him through my in-person follow-ups,*" I shared with inner Abby.

"*I cannot agree more. This is why I had said before, staying in Dubai is not helping your case. I think it's time to move back to Mumbai for good and see through the case. It will help us get a clearer picture of whether or not our Plan A would work. If it is headed towards failure, we will have to figure out a Plan B, the execution of which might also require you to be in Mumbai. However, I anticipate increased incidence of threats to Rey and you, once you make the move,*" inner Abby explained.

"*If moving back to Mumbai means expediting things, Mahesh's threats can't keep me from it. I can't keep fighting the case, just for the heck of it. The bigger objective is to punish him for his deeds and I will do whatever it takes to achieve that,*" I froze the plan.

Since I was going to be in Mumbai for a couple of more days and I was feeling dispirited due to the proceedings, I decided to pay a visit to Shalini who was back in Pune with Sia.

Shalini was working for an IT company in Pune. She used to leave for office at 8 a.m. in a cab, after seeing Sia off in the school bus. By 3 p.m., Sia's bus dropped her off at a creche that was barely a hundred metres from their apartment. Shalini got back from office at around 6 p.m., picked up Sia from the creche and walked back home.

"Hey, at office?" I called Shalini.

"Yes, what happened? All good?" she answered.

"Yeah, all good. How are you placed tomorrow?"

"Why do you ask? Are you planning to come to Pune?" she asked eagerly.

"Yeah, I have a couple of days with me and I don't have much to do tomorrow. So, I was contemplating driving down to Pune to catch up, if you have time."

"My life revolves around you, Abby. You tell me the time and I will manage. I can call in sick tomorrow if you want and we can spend the entire day together."

"No need to take an off. I have to get back to Mumbai the same day. So, we will have only a few hours. Why waste your leave for it? I can come down to some place near your office. That will save your time," I explained.

"Sure, what time?"

"Does 10 a.m. sound good?"

"10 a.m. it is. There is a mall right next to my office building. We can catch up over coffee there. I will send you the location on WhatsApp."

"Sure, see you tomorrow."

I drove to Pune the next morning in a rental car. I picked Shalini up at about 10.30 a.m. from her office building and drove into the mall beside it.

Like last time, there was no hug or handshake. She met me with a smile that could kill, and deeply engaging, heavenly eyes that could drown you in them if you managed to survive the smile. Like always, she looked stunning, this time in a black floral dress.

"Tired after the drive?" she asked as we made ourselves comfortable on the couch kept in the mall atrium. Since it wasn't 11 a.m. yet, the shops in the mall were still to open their shutters.

"You look beautiful," I ignored her question.

"Thank you!" she blushed.

"Any updates on the case?" she asked.

"Thanks to the sluggish system with an equally lazy lawyer, I am not happy with the way things are moving," I summarized what I had told her over call the previous day.

"So, what now?"

"I am coming back to India," I broke the news.

"Wow! That's great! But..."

"But what?"

"Will it help, and more importantly, will it be safe?"

"You don't want me to return?"

"If there is a list of people who want you back in India, I will be on top of that list. I am just scared for you and Rey. In India, you will be within Mahesh's reach and he can harm you guys. I don't want anything bad to happen," she said.

"Whatever happens, I will face it."

"Just think it through once more."

"You know when I decide anything, it is final. No one can change my decision."

"Who would know it better? When are you coming back?"

"In a couple of months or so. I will need to finalize a place to stay in Mumbai before that."

"But you already have an apartment in Mumbai, right?"

"Yeah, but I can't stay there. I don't want all of Myra's memories forcing themselves back into our lives. That might push me back into my shell and I really can't afford to do that at this point of time, when I desperately want justice for her."

"I understand. Like I said, staying in Mumbai might be a little risky given that Mahesh also stays there. Why don't you consider Pune? It is a nice city, it is close to Mumbai and is much safer. Besides that, I am in Pune and can help you out with everything," Shalini advised.

"Keep your friends close and enemies closer. Heard of that?" I shot down her idea.

I could read her mind and guess why she wanted me in Pune. I was aware of her love for me and her end game. I liked her too. But I had a bigger fish to fry at that time. Thoughts about spending our lives together under one roof had to wait, at least until I ensured Myra's culprit rotted for the rest of his life, surrounded by concrete and iron.

"I would have loved to move to Pune, but it will defeat the purpose of moving back from Dubai if I shift to any city other than Mumbai," I tried to explain.

"I agree. Let me know if you need any help with the house-hunting."

"Thanks Shalini! How is your work, by the way?"

"It's fine. What about yours? Resumed writing?"

"Not yet."

"You are such a gifted writer. You should write. Your readers must be waiting for your next blockbuster," she said.

"I guess I am living my next novel. I will start writing soon and it seems you will play an important character in it."

"I can't wait for it!"

After about two hours of constant blabbering, I decided to take her leave, but I believe she wanted to spend more time with me. So, she offered to come with me till the outskirts of Pune. From there, I would head towards Mumbai and she would take a cab back to her office.

Within five minutes of sitting in the car, she made the first move because she knew I wouldn't. She grabbed my left hand with her right one and entwined her fingers between mine. I felt the surge of hormones within me, kindling the desire to kiss her hand, followed by her lips, but the inner Abby held the reins tight. Though we locked our gaze multiple times, I avoided an extended eye contact, lest I would have again lost myself in her and my rented car would have witnessed some soft porn by the side of some isolated road in Pune.

"Your touch sends waves of current through my body," she said and I smiled back in reply.

Soon, we reached the city outskirts where I dropped her. I could not leave her alone to fetch a cab. So, I booked an Uber for her and parted ways with her only after seeing her off in the cab.

On my way back, I couldn't help but ruminate on our meeting that was kind of sweet. Her smallest of actions like coming with me to drop me off or holding my hand continuously for forty minutes while I drove, were striking the dormant chord of love in my heart. I don't know whether it was right or wrong, but it definitely felt good. I too, wanted to spend some more time with her and I could have, but I decided to bid goodbye because I was terrified of the guilt that would follow if I got expressive with my liking or love (maybe) during my extended hours with her. I left for Dubai the next day.

The next hearing happened in February and the case gained some momentum, but in the opposite direction. I was rigorously grilled about my relationship with Myra and her life insurance policy details were sought, as if it was my plot to get her killed. I was also questioned why it was more important for me to collect my novel from the printing press on the eventful day than taking her to the sonography clinic, thus forcing me to tell the court about our fight due to Shalini. As soon as Shalini's name came up, the court put a big question mark on the health of our (Myra and my) relationship and issued summon for Shalini to be present in the next hearing.

Mahesh's attorney was cunning, but a proficient and an experienced lawyer adept at turning around cases and he did the same here. He effortlessly turned the case on its head and portrayed me as the mastermind behind Myra's murder, citing my extramarital affair with Shalini and me being the beneficiary of Myra's life insurance policy payout of five crores. Shalini's divorce further fortified his claim. The defense alleged that I hired a thug to execute my coup de maître using Mahesh's (a high profile man's) car's registration number to fool the system. Shalini was labelled my accomplice in the crime.

As the defense attorney's allegation with logical arguments unfurled before me, I was dumbfounded and could only stare back in disbelief. It was a perfect example of how a straightforward case could be twisted and backfired at the complainant with believable motives. If I were a neutral spectator in the hearing, I would have been easily coerced into believing that I orchestrated my wife's murder, given the attorney's smooth arguments that fit in perfectly like pieces of a jigsaw puzzle. So, I could not blame the judge for attaching weight to it and wanting to dig deeper to explore that angle. That's how law is. In the eyes of the law, anyone can be the suspect if there is a justifiable motive, which was clearly present in my case.

When Shalini came to know about the summon, she was as thunderstruck as me, if not more. I was expecting her to be disquiet because of the unwanted carry-ons of headache that a court summon is loaded with, but the intensity of her panic surpassed my expectations.

"I am sorry that your name got dragged into this, Shalini. But there is nothing to worry," I was embarrassed because she got embroiled into my mess unintentionally.

"How do I not worry about this? You very well know about getting sucked into these court cases and that too, as a suspect for murder," she was filled with consternation.

"Worry is one thing, fear is another and I sense fear in you. Why are you scared? It is not possible for the defense attorney to corroborate his claim with any credible evidence and when there is no such evidence, there is no merit to his allegation in the eyes of the law. Come to think of it, it is just a way to digress the case and buy some time for themselves. I will work with my attorney to get our chat history and call records in place."

"I am not scared! Do whatever Abby, but get me out of this," she begged.

"Trust me, I will do my best to weed you out of it in the next hearing itself. This is my battle and I will never let any harm get to you," I assured her.

On the shifting bit, there was no alternative other than immediately relocating back to Mumbai because the court ordered me to do so as I was the prime suspect now. The judge was kind enough to allow me a month to relocate, which was well before the next hearing in April.

Instead of returning to Dubai right after the hearing, I stayed back in Mumbai for a week to look for a rented apartment. Despite being thrown off-track with the news of her summon, Shalini helped in searching and shortlisting suitable properties for me to physically visit and close. It didn't take me long to finalize a humongous, fully-furnished four-bedroom apartment on the twenty-fourth floor of a high-rise in a posh society in Lokhandwala, the same vicinity I owned my previous apartment in.

As per my requirement, the apartment was in an upscale society that boasted of housing quite a few Bollywood celebrities. I wanted a high-profile society to live in because such societies had super-tight security, something that was top priority for me because of Rey. That it costed me five lakhs of rent per month didn't compare against the value of our safety.

The moment I had seen the apartment and the breathtaking, meditative view of the skyline its huge balcony offered, it had my heart and the search for my new abode had ended right then and there. It had a monstrous living room. Each of the four bedrooms came with a powder-room. The master bedroom was a suite in itself, with an additional living room and a study of its own. It had massive French windows all around that stretched from the floor to the ceiling, giving it an open feel. The interiors were sumptuous and tastefully done with fancy lighting and expensive furniture, much to my liking. Myra would have loved it as much as I did.

With Rey getting impatient due to my prolonged absence, I rushed back to Dubai immediately. It took me about three more weeks to wrap up things there and be back in Mumbai for good, just in time before the court's deadline in March.

Since I also needed a set of wheels to get around in the city, I got myself a swanky, new BMW 5 series that had always been on my radar. In the midst of so much turmoil and stress in our lives, Rey and I needed something to cheer us up and our stunning, carbon black Bimmer did just that.

My parents had mixed feelings about my return due to their inherent fear of Mahesh. They thought he had diverted the case in order to force my return to Mumbai where he would be more in control of things to torment me. Since Dad was a famous educationist who had a powerful hold in Bihar with contacts in the police as well as the State Government, he wanted Rey to shift to Patna, instead of staying with me in Mumbai, a suggestion I politely refused at that time.

On one hand, I worked with my attorney to collate all the evidences like WhatsApp and Facebook chats between me and Shalini along with our call records, while on the other, I worked with Shalini to hire a full-time maid to take care of Rey so that I could leave him at home whenever I had to go out for any important work related to the case or otherwise. Hiring a maid would also free us from the compulsion of Mom travelling to take care of Rey every time I had to be present for the hearing.

As instructed by Shalini, I sourced some profiles of maids from the building's security and forwarded them to her to interview and finalize. She conducted video interviews with them when they visited my new home.

For me, the maid's ability to click with Rey and take care of him with her heart was more important than her looks. That's the reason I gave every shortlisted candidate a chance to be with him for about fifteen minutes and observed her behaviour. After evaluating seven candidates, Simmi made the final cut.

Simmi was a twenty-year-old, five-feet tall, skinny, Marathi girl with fair complexion and limited linguistic abilities. Though another candidate seemed better with a working knowledge of spoken English, Shalini outrightly rejected her because she was a divorcee, was over thirty-five years old and had a curvy body – ticking all the check boxes for her rejection.

For a maid who would stay 24x7 with a lone man under the same roof, I believe Simmi's skinny built tilted the scale in her favour because Shalini knew 'skinny' was not my type and I would maintain my distance. Shalini had clearly started growing possessive about me. With the bigger problem of my court case at hand and limited time, I didn't want to fuss about her decision because I wanted to finalize a maid at the earliest and Simmi wasn't that bad.

Regarding Rey's schooling, his safety could have been compromised if we sent him to school. Both, Shalini and I, were on the same page with respect to home-schooling him, at least for a year.

For the hearing in April, Shalini had to travel to Mumbai. She called her parents to Pune to take care of Sia while she would be away. To avoid causing undue stress to them, she told them she was going to Mumbai for some official work.

"Hey, all set to come to Mumbai?" I called her a couple of days before the hearing.

"Kind of! Mom-Dad are here. Packing is almost done. The hotel booking is also confirmed," she replied.

"You can stay at my house, if you want," my offer had no sexual insinuation.

"Are you playing from Mahesh's side?" she asked sarcastically.

"As in?" I wanted her to elaborate.

"The defense is trying to prove there was something between us, which is why we planned Myra's murder. You want to add gasoline to that fire?" she explained to me.

"Oh yeah, you are right."

"Though I so wish I could stay at your place, let's avoid it and save ourselves the hassle of defending a barrage of questions on our growing proximity recently. We should wait until we get off the hook."

"I am with you on it. Which hotel are you staying at?"

"Sofitel in BKC. It is better to stay a little away from you. Let's also refrain from meeting."

"As you wish, Shalini. See you in court then. Don't be nervous; I will get you out of my mess," I assured her.

"I guess anxiety is getting the better of me, but I do trust you."

It took the next two hearings, one in April and the other in June to finally get vindicated, but not before a rigorous deep-diving by the court into the allegations made by the defense.

Before Myra's death, Shalini and my interactions were limited. Our chats were formal and friendly with no stench of murder-plotting of my own wife. There was also no inkling of our affair. No call records were found and the judge was convinced there was no foul play from our side. Throughout both the hearings, Shalini looked abnormally pale with trepidation and was perennially edgy, making my guilt burst through the roof, but I was confident we would be out of the ambit of the baseless assertion of the defense attorney unscathed because he couldn't possibly have any relevant evidence.

After the hearing, Shalini and I parted ways without much interaction. She left for her hotel, saying she would call me while I returned home to Rey, who was being looked after decently well by Simmi.

"Thank you for keeping your promise, Abby," she called after reaching the hotel.

"Don't embarrass me, Shalini. You had nothing to do with the case and should have been kept away from it. All the panic it caused you is on me and I am very sorry for it," I apologized.

"It wasn't your fault. Forget about it," she pacified me.

"Won't you show me your new home? I have only seen it in pictures and video calls," she continued.

"Yeah, of course. I thought we were not supposed to meet, which is why I didn't ask you. Can you come home tonight for dinner?" I offered.

"The court dismissed the affair angle today. So, no barriers now; I can come. More than seeing your apartment and spending some time with you, I want to meet Rey. It has been long overdue."

"Come then. By the way, he knows about you," I told her.

"What? What have you told him?"

"The truth."

"Can you elaborate?"

"I have showed him your photos and told him that you were my girlfriend who I loved a lot, but I got dumped," I said.

"He is a kid for god's sake. It's not the age to know about these things. And can you please stop saying that I dumped you? It makes me cringe with guilt."

"I have told him we are very good friends now and our break-up was destined to happen."

"He might be having a very negative impression of me because I hurt his dad who is everything for him."

"He did think you were cruel, but not anymore. He is aware that you have always been there for him and me ever since Myra left us. And, he thinks you are beautiful."

"So cute of him. I can't wait to hug him."

"By what time should I expect you?"

"It is 5 already. I need to freshen up and get ready which would take an hour. Not sure how much time it would take to wade through the peak hour traffic to get to your place."

"Approximately an hour. So, you can be here by 7," I calculated.

"Cool, I will see you and my baby at 7."

"Your baby?"

"Yeah, don't you know I have two babies now – Sia and Rey?" her comment won me over.

There was a noticeable impatience within me and a spring in my step as I walked to and fro waiting for her, constantly cracking my knuckles, completely unaware of what our casual catch-up would turn into.

CHAPTER 7

Location: Mumbai
Time: June 2019

Shalini reached my place by 7.30 p.m. She looked divine in a tight-fitted, gold-outlined, royal blue kameez paired with a matching Patiala salwar and a dupatta. As soon as I saw her, my eyes plumped up with hearts. With about four-inch heels, she was almost as tall as me. As we hugged, I could smell her Gucci perfume radiating its premium fragrance.

"You look gorgeous," I whispered in her ear.

"And you look hot in black!" she counter-complimented me with her eyes searching for Rey.

"He is inside with Simmi. Go say hi to him. Let's see if he recognizes you," I said, but she was already on her way to find him. I followed.

"Hi handsome!" Shalini greeted Rey.

"Hi," Rey replied and continued playing with his Lego blocks while Simmi smiled at Shalini and nodded her head to greet her.

"Do you know who I am?" Shalini asked Rey.

"You are Shalini," Rey was too smart to not recognize her.

"That's right, my little genius," Shalini commended.

"Shalini aunty," I corrected Rey.

"Oh, let it be. Let him call me Shalini. It will make me feel younger," Shalini said.

Like a child, she sat on the floor beside Rey and started playing with him while I made myself comfortable on the couch to spectate their burgeoning camaraderie that continued when she fed him dinner an hour later.

Rey could sense vibrations from people and was always very clear with his feelings. He dealt in binary – it was either 0 or 1, he either liked people or disliked them; there was no golden mean for him. If he didn't like anyone, he would say it on his face without deodorizing his words. His feelings always showed on his face and in his expressive eyes. So, I was a little skeptical about him meeting Shalini. What if he didn't like her and told her directly so? However, throughout his time with Shalini, he was more gleeful than he had ever been since Myra's demise, slaughtering my apprehension away.

When the two most important people in your life gel with each other, it is a huge moment of relief. Rey's approval of Shalini as my best friend (at least for now) mattered a lot and I had already got an inkling of it. An icing on the cake was when Rey shockingly asked me for permission to let Shalini put him to sleep.

"Daddy, can Shalini aunty put me to sleep tonight?" Rey asked with utmost innocence.

"Don't trouble aunty. Otherwise, she won't come home next time," I told Rey.

"Abby, can I put Rey to sleep tonight?" Shalini asked me in the same tone as Rey's.

"You can relax and have your me-time na, Daddy. You will not even have to think about what bedtime story to tell me. Shalini aunty will tell me the story tonight, right aunty?" Rey tried to convince me.

"Of course, I will tell my baby a story," Shalini pulled him in her arms and kissed him.

"Alright, but sleep quickly and don't pester her," I instructed Rey as the mother-son duo hopped their way to the bedroom.

Every night after Myra's death, Rey slept with no one in the world but me, except the nights I couldn't be with him when I was in Mumbai for the hearing and he was in Dubai with Mom. So, I was taken aback by his request.

When I did a surprise-check on them to see if things were in control, I witnessed another first in the dim light of the night lamp. Standing in the doorway, I saw a motherless child cuddled carefreely into a mother's arms, cocooned from the world's harsh realities and savouring every word of her story. Not even for a moment did it feel she was not his biological mother, the love and the connection between them were so evident and unblemished. I just froze there at the door, overwhelmed with emotions until tears in my eyes showed up to witness the display of love between a mother and her son.

"What happened Daddy?" Rey's voice pierced through my thoughts.

"Sleep, sleep," I walked off wiping my tears, without engaging in any conversation to prevent Shalini and Rey from noticing my wobbly voice and moistened eyes.

Feeling choked and out of breath, I walked into the balcony to get some fresh air. I was a mixed bag of emotions. I was happy for that moment because Rey was relishing catching up on the warmth, love and security of a mother that he had missed for almost four years. At the same time, I was extremely heartbroken because I was missing Myra and was feeling pity for Rey and myself. I was also worried about how I would handle him when he woke up the next morning to Shalini's absence. That would pain his heart, which in turn would pain mine.

Amidst my emotional battle, I felt familiar hands slide from both my sides to my stomach and embrace me from behind. It was Shalini who was back after putting Rey to sleep. As her warm body squeezed against mine, all my thoughts miraculously vanished into thin air. I held her hands gently to acknowledge her hug as they slithered up to my chest and clasped my body tightly, inevitably making me feel her bosoms on my back. As she breathed heavily on the back of my neck, I felt a sense of quietude and relief, bereft of all thoughts.

"What happened?" she asked.

"Nothing, I was just soaking in the view from the balcony. I have never really had the chance and the mental bandwidth to do so," I replied.

"You think I didn't notice?" she caught me.

"Your hug has rendered me motionless. If you have noticed something move in my otherwise immobile body, it is because of increased blood circulation stimulated by your body and is completely involuntary," I tried to evade her question with my witless humour.

"I will deal with that movement appropriately at the right time. First things, first. When you came to the room, why did you have tears in your eyes? Missing Myra?" she hit the nail on the head. She knew me more than I had thought.

"The tears just came out on their own. I don't know why," I replied.

"Think and tell me," she was not ready to let it go so easily.

"When I saw Rey and you interacting, it felt like a son bonding with his mother. I haven't seen him so happy in the last four years. That filled me with emotions and pushed the tears out. Thank you for this moment, Shalini."

"I loved playing mother to him. He is a great kid and you are a great father, Abby."

"But no matter how great a father I am, I can never be his mother. The love between a son and his mother is different, and that's something I can never give him. I don't know how I will handle him if he wakes up in the middle of the night looking for you or when he wakes up tomorrow morning and asks for you. I can't see him sad," I said.

"If it makes you a little relieved, I can stay overnight. But that will be on the condition that I sleep with Rey. So, he will wake up to me tomorrow."

"Thank you so much!" I turned around to hug her, heart-to-heart.

"Now, let's move to the movable part of your body that is now poking me," she said and held my manhood, sending a burst of energy to all parts of my body.

By the time my brain could think and send the signal to my mouth to respond to her in words, it was already engrossed in kissing her, while my hands, after getting the go-ahead from her action, slipped down and squeezed her plump derriere.

There was no fear of her family intruding our privacy this time. Rey hadn't slept the entire day and was too tired to wake up, at least for the next four to five hours. Simmi was in the servant's room. There were chances that she might peep into our intimate space and the news might spread in my society like wild fire through the network of maids; but I frankly didn't care. Those who would want to gossip about it and paint a bad image of me would do it anyway. So mentally, I was free from all such inhibitions as they weighed little against my sacred union with Shalini.

As we both breathed heavily down one another, I lifted her up in my arms to take her to my other bedroom without wasting a minute. Amidst the sudden surge of energy and the subsequent temptation to sprint to the bedroom, fling her on the bed and jump onto her, I controlled my horses and carried her patiently to the bedroom.

Once we reached the room, I carefully made her stand on the floor. As our lips refused to disengage, she unbuckled my belt and pulled my trousers down in tandem with me getting rid of my shirt. Our lips unlocked for a few seconds, when I helped her undress her kameez while she helped me get rid of my trousers completely, and locked back in for our tongues to continue on their exploratory journeys.

To my irritation, when I tried to undo the cord of her salwar, it got stuck in a knot. My impatient mind was toying with the idea of ripping off the salwar or cutting it with scissors, but thankfully, her hands came to its rescue, sensing my violent intentions and untied its cord to let it fall on the floor.

I quickly bolted the door behind us and turned on the bedside lamp to see how god had made her and make love to her while looking into her magical eyes. I pushed her onto the bed, got on top of her and freed her of her unwanted innerwear so that our bodies could connect without any third thing in between, not even a thread of fabric. I couldn't help but marvel at her angelic body that gleamed even in the dim lighting of the room.

I wanted to be familiar with every contour of her body that I felt was mine since forever, but had got lost for years because of destiny's blunder. Destiny was now trying to make up for it. As I crawled all over her to explore every single part of her body, kissing each part and relishing its taste as it came my way, she quivered but didn't try to stop me.

To stamp her rights over me that she had now certainly established, she pushed me onto her side, climbed on top of me and skimmed over my body to give me a taste of how she felt when I did the same a few moments ago. Our actions conveyed I owned her and she owned me back - mentally, physically and spiritually.

I frantically opened the bedside table drawer with my right hand while my body was still pinned under her and pretended to fetch a condom that I knew wasn't there. Why would it be? I never thought I would need it, given that I had taken a vow of celibacy since Myra's death, a vow that Shalini was vigorously blowing out sitting on my chest with her back almost smothering my face while I was admiring her behind and doing indescribable things to intensify her aroused state.

She swiveled around to face me, held my hand and whispered breathing down my face, "Don't! I want to feel you inside me without that thing you are looking for."

She kissed and laid on top of me, surrendering herself for the ultimate step. Looking into her divine, hypnotic and expressive eyes, I impaled her, leading us both into a state of euphoria. Mumbai's humidity had washed the perfume off her body with her sweat, and my covert decision to not switch on either the fan or the air-conditioner helped the cause. I wanted that because I needed her body's fragrance all over me.

The feel of her desirable body brushing against mine, coupled with her intoxicating, untainted body fragrance and the sweet flavour of her mouth that I could access through our lips intertwined into one, turned me on to the hilt and switched on all the right buttons. I don't know about her, but I was in heaven. Her thick, untied hair covered the sides of our faces and curtained us from the rest of the world. There was only me, Shalini, and the surreal feeling of our soulful union, nothing else.

Our bodies climaxed one after another and shuddered uncontrollably as it happened. In the frenzy of her orgasm, she bit my lips hard and dug her nails into my head, almost pulling my hair before collapsing with a gurgle like an animal being slaughtered.

"I love you," the words exhaled out of my mouth along with my breath.

"I love you too," she whispered back.

We lay on the bed for some time for our heart rate to become normal, before washing together. It was a little embarrassing to be in a state of nature with my former classmate in the lighted washroom, but it was mysteriously exciting. As we stole glances at each other's bodies, we realized we hadn't had enough of one another. It was like when our stomach is full but the food is so luscious that we want to eat more. The second round lasted much longer, leaving us completely defeated.

It would be human to compare the love-making with Shalini, my first love, to that with Myra, my ultimate love, but would also be criminal to do so. Let me just say that the gratification it brought seemed unprecedented and it was because of multiple reasons. First, Shalini was my first love and 'first love' always has a special place in the heart. Second, it was something that was pending since forever. Third, Shalini was irresistibly attractive, at least to me.

"Nobody has ever made love to me the way you did. You made me feel so desirable," Shalini complimented as we both stared at the ceiling lying next to each other on the bed.

"Thank you! By the way, how many people have made love to you?" I joked and got an instant shot of her elbow into the side of my ribs.

"Ouch! I was just joking."

"I don't like such jokes," she was serious.

"Sorry, I didn't mean it that way," I turned and kissed her on the forehead as she continued to rest her head on my arm.

"It's ok," she snuggled into me.

"You remember, I had told you about the planchette me and my friends had done in my college?" she asked.

"Don't you think this is an inappropriate time to talk about ghost stuff? Are you a witch or something?" I was surprised. Who talks about ghosts during such an intimate moment?

"Stop crapping, there is a connection. Tell me na, you remember?" she repeated her question.

"Ok, tell me about it."

"When we had called the spirit, we had asked it a number of questions. One of the things the spirit had told us was that one of your IIT batchmates named Veer would marry one of my batchmates who was also present that night with us. That time, I had checked with you if a guy named Veer existed at your college and you had confirmed it. You knew him."

"Yeah, I recall that now. What's the connection?" I was curious.

"I had also asked the spirit about our marriage and it had replied in the affirmative. It was always there, engraved in destiny that it would happen. I didn't know the journey to it would be such a long haul. Though we have not married each other yet, we are unknowingly cruising on that road and I have a strong feeling we would, one day."

"That's creepy, to say the least," I ignored the latter part of what she said.

"Tell me one thing, Abby," she wouldn't let me off the topic.

"What?"

"Few months or years down the line, whenever you are mentally ready, would you like to spend the rest of your life with me as my lawfully wedded husband?"

"I can't believe you are proposing to me, and that too, in such a unique way."

"You can assume that."

"Shalini, I love you and I care for you. I can ignore the fact, but I can't deny it. Having said that, the topmost priority for me is getting justice for Myra. Answering your question truthfully and committing right now will digress me from my objective and might also put you and Sia in danger because I am up against vicious and powerful people. Our closeness will increase and show. The moment these guys come to know of it, they will come after you. It will make me weaker and more vulnerable. Please understand, I cannot give an answer right now."

"I got my answer, in an equally twisted way. It's a 'yes' but I understand you need time and I will give you that. I will wait for you, even if I have to wait until we are sixty years old."

"That's sweet, but let's just live in the moment," I hugged her.

"Cool! Talking about the case, do you think you will get justice?"

"I used to think I would, but now, my trust in the system is wavering. Let's see. What do you think?"

"Should I tell you what I honestly feel or what you would like to hear?"

"Of course, I would want to know your unbiased opinion."

"Honestly, I am not too hopeful. It is a well-known fact that the system is corrupt from top to bottom. Mahesh has deep pockets, enough to bribe the judge and the police. Sorry to say, but the odds are stacked against you. Besides that, the risk of losing your or your loved ones' lives is not something worth signing up for. There is an inherent fear in you, in me and in all of us close to you, though nobody tells you to your face. Who knows, the turning of tables in the case to make us the accused might happen again? What if your parents are made the accused this time?

"If you still haven't realized, the case has taken maximum toll on you and there is high probability that all of this might be for nothing because of our unscrupulous judicial system. This case is a constant pain in the neck that is coming in way of your personal and professional lives. Tell me, what work have you done in the last three to four years? Nothing! You are an author and you have not written a word in these years. It is all because of this case."

"Stop beating around the bush. What are you driving at?" I was losing my patience.

"I think you should withdraw the case."

"Are you kidding me?" I was surprised.

"You asked me for my honest opinion and I gave it to you."

"It is now that the case has gained some momentum. How can I pull the plug on it? I get your point, but I want to take my chances. I will not let that bastard escape so easily."

"Give it a thought, consider all points and then take a call. I will be with you in whatever you decide."

Shalini had raised valid points and it actually made sense to withdraw the case, but that would mean a more dangerous and annihilating Plan B would have to be mandatorily put into effect. I didn't have a plan B ready, but thinking a level deeper, if I had to deliver justice myself, I would go by my *Law of Revenge*, according to which:

"*Revenge MUST be extracted in equal measure, no matter what.*"

So, whatever details the plan would entail, the objective of bringing Mahesh to book would have to be executed illegally by me and that would most certainly land me in jail or might even deprive me of my life. Harming someone would also not come naturally to me. I was a common man, not some Bollywood hero. I wasn't ready for it. I wasn't born for it. It wasn't my *dharma*. That was not the purpose god had sent me to earth for. He had sent me to write interesting novels, build businesses and help people. I didn't want to go down that irreversible, unlawful road that ended either in prison or in grave, which is why I subconsciously didn't want to withdraw the case and wished to take my chances with Plan A. But remember? The more I ran away from something, the more it caught up with me. First, it was studies and now, it was Plan B. The thoughts of Plan B started making me sick to my stomach.

"Hey, are you still with me?" Shalini's voice interrupted my thoughts.

"I was thinking about something," I replied.

"Don't think about anything but me right now," she said as her hand caressed my chest, suggesting she wanted to go for the hat-trick.

Still somewhat 'high' on her beauty and 'dry' on the stressful thoughts about Plan B, I made love to her for the third time in a row. It was exhausting, but exceptionally fulfilling, though it ended up giving us both a bad pain in our lower abdomen.

After cleaning up, Shalini went to sleep alongside Rey and I surrendered to my sleep in the bedroom that had seen it all that night, but not before realizing that I had gone too far with her without the license to do so from inner Abby. His rebellious voice had got dissipated in the heat of our bodies during our passionate love-making marathon. He would probably make me jump to death for what I had done. To save my face and avoid a direct confrontation, I deliberately chose not to engage with him that night.

A couple of hours into my sleep, it seemed someone opened the door, walked in and sat on the chair right in front of the bed.

"Wake up," a female voice ordered as I struggled to open my eyes and sit up, only to peer at a woman sitting right across and staring in my face.

"Had fun?" she asked while I narrowed my eyes to recognize her.

"Mmmyra...?" I stammered as a chill ran down my spine causing goosebumps.

"You thought you would bang her and I wouldn't come to know? I had told you I would always be around, even when you would be sleeping with other women after my death," she was upset.

"Nnnoo, it...it happened in the moment of the heat...I mean, in the heat of the moment," I was fumbling with my words.

"Out of all the women in the world, you had sex with Shalini? Why?" she deliberately used the word 'sex' instead of 'love-making'.

"I am sorry, it just happened," I noticed sweat appearing on my forehead despite the air-conditioner set at twenty degrees Celsius.

"I knew you always loved her. You must be so happy I am gone from your life. You got your shot at living your fantasy of fucking your first love. The road to her is clear. When is the wedding?"

"Thanks for the taunt when I have also been perennially sad and been slogging relentlessly to get you justice for the last four years. How convenient of you to only focus on tonight and jibe at me!"

"I haven't taunted you yet sweetheart, but I will, after your fourth and my first round because you will have to do me now, you sexually-starved animal," she screeched and lunged onto me like a zombie, pinning me down on the bed.

I tried to scream for help, but found no voice, as if she had pressed the mute button in me. I attempted to free myself from under her, but in vain. And then, I woke up. It was a nightmare!

Though I was relieved to realize it was just a bad dream, my horror didn't end there. I was unable to open my eyes. My body felt paralyzed and I could not move my hands or legs, not even my torso. I was fully awake from inside and if anyone would have seen me from outside, he would have seen my eyeballs moving restlessly underneath my closed eyelids. My heart was palpitating and my breaths had become shorter and faster. Getting my head around what was going on was secondary; I had to first gain back control over my incapacitated, helpless body.

I mustered all my strength, and with a sudden jerk, turned to my right to make myself fall over the edge of the bed. The trick worked and I fell on the floor, the impact reviving me. I was covered in cold sweat. There was no one else around. The bed and the chair were also empty, much to my relief.

I glanced at the closed but unbolted door with my myopic eyes. Before slumping into my bed, I had purposely left the door unbolted so that Rey could find me if he woke up in the middle of the night. For some reason, I felt like putting on my spectacles and checking the door. To my horror, the door was bolted from inside! It literally knocked the piss out of me and sent incessant shivers down my entire body, making the hairs on my body stand straight up like those of a porcupine.

I had always been a firm believer in ghosts. You could ridicule me or call me names for believing in them, but my belief on them would not budge. God may or may not exist, but ghosts do.

There are two types of people in this world. First, who can sense vibrations and second, who can't. Supernatural beings like ghosts have vibrations associated with them and the first type of people have the innate gift (or curse) to sense their presence through those vibrations, even if they don't want to. The ghosts also try to make their presence felt more to this type. Such people often hear sounds in the dead of the night or catch a glimpse of someone standing or walking from the corner of their eyes, but when they turn around to have a look, they see no one. When they sleep at night, they often feel someone tickling or touching their feet or some insect crawling on their soles or legs because of which they prefer sleeping with a blanket or a sheet covering their legs (even in summers) to avoid the eerie feeling. They get goosebumps for no reason or sense a foul smell all of a sudden, indicating the presence of a supernatural being very close to them. Luckily or unluckily, I fell in this category and had enough ghostly experiences under my belt to prove their existence.

With trembling legs struggling to walk my body, I managed to open the door and wobble my way to Rey's room. Shalini was fast asleep on one side of Rey. I quietly slid into his blanket from the other side. It was cardinal for me to rule out Myra's ghost coming over, to maintain my sanity. Lying sideways facing away from Rey, with arms wrapped around my bent knees, I started putting logic to the incident, feigning disbelief in ghosts, like a true science sceptic.

Myra loved me and if she had the power to visit me during my objectionable encounter with another woman, she must have also had the power to visit me at all other times when I missed her so much that I wanted to end my life; but she didn't. However, negative emotions like anger are more capable of eliciting reactions than positive ones like love and we all know, *Hell hath no fury like a woman scorned.* Imagine what a scorned woman ghost could do.

I was baffled as to whether it was a nightmare or Myra was actually there. Somewhere in my heart, there was that guilt conscience of sleeping with Shalini, which perhaps coupled with our discussion on ghosts to result in the nightmare.

But what about the bolted door? I started thinking of possible scenarios to justify it. Unfortunately, there was just one possibility! I got up in my sleep and bolted the door. I had never sleep-walked in my life of over three decades. Sleeptalk yes, but sleepwalk, a sure-shot no. But there's always a first time.

Next up was explaining someone clamping me down on the bed and my body refusing to obey my brain's orders. It could have been because I got too involved in my nightmare to feel everything in real and the feeling lingered on even after I woke up. I was also physically drained after the sensual episode with Shalini, which is why my body would have been too tired to move. Alternatively, there could be some issue in my brain that caused a kind of seizure and it would require immediate medical check-up by a neurologist.

While I was combating my state of delirium that had spooked my sleep off, Rey turned and hugged me from behind, as if he sensed my restlessness. His touch almost instantly tranquilized me into deep sleep.

I woke up late the next morning with a terrible migraine. Everyone else had already woken up. Shalini was ready to leave after feeding Rey his breakfast.

"Hey, good morning! Slept well?" Shalini asked.

"Good morning Daddy," Rey added.

"Good morning. I can't say I slept too well," I replied.

"Did you sleepwalk into our room?" Shalini smiled as Simmi's ears got activated. She would have a busy day cooking stories about me and Shalini, and sharing them within her network.

"I had a horrifying dream and started feeling uneasy. So, I came to your room," I was embarrassed.

"You want to talk about it?" she was concerned.

"Not important," I brushed the issue off.

I thanked Shalini for coming over and spending time with me and Rey. Special mention to our marathon session that would seem wrong to many and right to some. For those who think I was right, we would be on the same page. Like I have always believed, right or wrong for anyone should never be decided by others. There is no rule book for it. If you think something is right, it is indeed right and vice versa. I told myself whatever happened was right for the moment and I should not feel sad thinking about it.

For those who think I was wrong, I am not god and so, I was well within my rights to be wrong at times, at least in non-fatal matters. Having said that, a tinge of guilt was certainly there and I knew it would bother me until I got justice for Myra. So, I decided I would abstain from any physical intimacy with Shalini until that time. Little did I know, I would have to smash my promise to smithereens and get into a guilt-free, uninhibited night of love and vengeance with her a few months later, thanks to what Myra was purportedly doing behind my back when she was alive.

CHAPTER 8

Location: Mumbai
Time: July 2019 - August 2019

After Shalini's departure, Rey felt a little low for a couple of days, but he was completely back to normal in a week. He and Shalini had carried on with their mother-son relationship over calls. He had his own phone through which they were also in touch over WhatsApp. I could see he missed her physical presence and longed to be with her, but he kept his emotions to himself and I didn't prod him with my questions because I wanted him to fight his own battles in life.

The case gained pace in the right direction in the August hearing, with the court asking us to provide proofs against Mahesh, the primary ones being CCTV footage of my previous society's main gate camera and the key eye-witnesses (the then security guards of my society) who would testify against him. The defense attorney argued that Mahesh was not present at the scene of accident when it happened and that he had five alibis who would confirm his location at a restaurant more than twenty kilometres away at the time of the accident. Both the sides were given time until the next hearing in October to present their respective evidences to buttress their claims.

My conversations with Shalini now happened over phone and WhatsApp multiple times during the day and she was aware of every single update on the case. I had not cut down on my emotional closeness to her because of the nightmare I had had. I had chosen to dismiss that episode of night terror as my hallucination and move on in life. Not that important, but my brain's MRI report had also turned up normal. Since nothing unusual recurred that could be attributed to anything supernatural, it fortified my assumption of the incident being a figment of my imagination though with some inexplicable and mysterious pointers that were harmless. Unless they affected my life, I wouldn't waste time on solving such innocuous mysteries; we all live with unresolved ones. However, like I had decided, I consciously avoided physical intimacy with her to focus on the case.

Shalini had been under some kind of perpetual stress that she had concealed from me, but an undercurrent of disquiet was always evident from her demeanour. At first, I thought it was the divorce case, then the separation from her husband and later, the court summon and other routine tensions. I felt she needed time to tide over her issues and so, refrained from asking her about it. But when it had been quite some time since her issues got settled and the undercurrent still persisted, I was forced to intervene. With multiple intimate moments that had brought us very close to each other, it made sense to do so. She was investing a lot emotionally into me and it was only fair on my part to ask and rid her of her troubles, if any.

"Can I ask you something?" I asked Shalini one day after our daily regimen of providing updates.

"Yeah, of course," she replied.

"Is there something bothering you?"

"No, just the usual. Office work and Sia."

"Rey and I also add to that."

"Not really. You guys are my stress-busters. Actually, the project I am working on is a little too tedious and demanding. When I come home, I have to take care of Sia's studies too. She is a bright child, but has started lagging behind her classmates."

"I can understand. But I feel there is something else that has been troubling you for a long time."

"Nothing else that I can think of."

"You had told me your life revolves around me; now, mine has started revolving around you. If there is anything bugging you, you need to tell me. I promise I will get you out of it. Is there any financial concern?"

"No, I earn a decent salary that is more than sufficient for both me and Sia. My parents are here with me in Pune and you know they are financially well-off. So, no such concern."

"Is Prashant causing any problem?" I asked further.

"No, he hasn't got in touch even once to meet Sia."

"Any threats from unknown people, probably working for Mahesh?"

"Come on Abby, stop it! I told you there is nothing else apart from work and Sia," she got terribly annoyed.

"I ask because I care, Shalini. There is no need to get fired up," I reasoned sternly.

"Sorry, my bad. I know you care for me. Trust me, you would be the first one I would tell if there was anything out of order in my life," she tried to explain.

"Did you think about withdrawing the case?" she continued.

"I am not withdrawing it."

"Why are you so adamant? The threats to you have increased in number and intensity. Don't take a chance with the lives of your loved ones just because of your ego, Abby. Not worth it."

"Ego or whatever, I have told you before and my decision remains the same. And if you decide to distance yourself from me because of it, I can understand."

"I don't know what to say. Anyway, let me call you once I reach Pune."

"Once you reach Pune? You are not in Pune?"

"Sorry, just missed telling you. I had come to Mumbai for some official work," she told me.

"You tell me every single bit about yourself, Shalini – the time you eat, bathe or teach Sia, the things you do every day, the places you go to, the shower gel and perfumes you use, etc. And you missed telling me about coming to Mumbai?"

"I told you, the project and Sia have drained me. I have been off, especially for the last few days. I am sorry, I forgot."

"If you don't want to meet me, I am fine with it."

"I will plan a leave from work next month and come to Mumbai to be with you. If you want, I will come right now. You know I love you more than anyone else. Don't doubt my love in any way."

Though I asked her not to turn around midway, she did and came back to Mumbai right then. She looked exhausted when she came home and I felt like such a douchebag for doubting her. Despite her worn down state, she looked exquisite. We didn't make love though I really wanted to, but we did make out for a few minutes that we got sans Rey (slightly against my resolve to maintain physical distance from her). Those few minutes were enough for her to blow my mind away with her kiss, touch and tears that flushed out all my doubts on her love, from my mind.

I apologized to her, to which she said there was no need. Since she had started getting calls from Sia asking when Shalini would return home because she was waiting for her, I decided to drop her off all the way to Pune in my car. Rey tagged along for the fun of travelling in his favourite car with his favourite person, Shalini. We dropped her off at her society's entrance and didn't go to her house because her parents were there. We stayed the night in a hotel and left for Mumbai early next morning.

Keeping Shalini's true love aside for a moment, despite her firm stand on having no critical concerns, I was somehow not convinced. I had lived enough to realize that my sixth sense was strong and I had a powerful intuition about something amiss that she was not telling me about. She undoubtedly loved me, but did she really miss telling me about coming to Mumbai or she deliberately hid it from me? Was she on an official trip or she had some other agenda? Was she in some serious trouble and was keeping it from me because she thought I already had a lot on my plate?

I was worried about her well-being and safety. I had genuinely started caring for her and would annihilate anyone who dared to harm her in any way. But she had slammed the door shut on the face of my questions. Apart from her, only time held the key to that door and I knew I would have to wait patiently for it to get unlocked. However, that only led to the problem getting bigger with worst possible solutions needed in place to take care of it, but all for the best. I wouldn't have had it any other way.

Regarding quitting the case, had I succumbed to Shalini's persistent pressure to do so, it would have definitely saved me the hassle of being abducted a month later, but wouldn't have stirred up a hornet's nest that led to some life-altering moments in our lives.

CHAPTER 9

Location: Mumbai
Time: September 2019

What Mahesh told me about Myra had stunned me and spun my life into another orbit. My brain had gone numb and I was unable to think clearly. The shock of an unwanted abduction had further incapacitated my mind.

He said Myra was clandestinely doing something that she would be ashamed of. So ashamed that it would make him say she might have attempted suicide by jumping in front of his car? What had happened in *her* life? It was not his or her life between me and Myra. It was always *our* life. When did it turn to hers alone? And he claimed to have proof of it? What kind of proof? Could it just be a bluff or it had some meat in it? She would never jump in front of the car to commit suicide, definitely not when Rey was with her. So, that part was a bluff for sure and even Mahesh was speculating about it. Maybe, he said it just to emphasize the intensity of the ignominy. But what about the embarrassment part? There is no smoke without fire and if the point had indeed come up, there was definitely something about Myra that I was missing. I tried to think with my remnant thinking ability.

"I have nothing personal with you. Mahesh sir is way too powerful to be within your bounds. Whoever is gone cannot come back. You need to protect whoever is with you right now. My advice is to agree to whatever he is saying," Bhide dropped me at the entrance of my building at around 2 p.m., about seven hours after my kidnapping, with his final words.

"Daddy... where were you? I had been looking for you," Rey hugged me as soon as I entered the house.

"Had some urgent work beta. Just give me some time to normalize; you can watch YouTube videos until then," I hugged him back.

"Bhaiya, are you ok?" Simmi was concerned.

"Yeah, I am fine. Just get me a bottle of cold water," I walked outside into the balcony to get some air.

I sipped some water from the bottle and poured the remaining on my head before sinking into my balcony couch. What I had gone through had stupefied me and I felt I needed someone to help me think clearly. There was just one person I could call, the person who was fluidly dethroning inner Abby to become my go-to person for advice.

"Where are you, Abby? I have been trying your number since morning. I have been worried for you. Couldn't you drop a message before turning off your phone for such an extended period of time? You didn't even inform Simmi or Rey where you were going," Shalini was clearly stressed and spoke at length before I could say a word.

"I need you, Shalini," even the strongest of people have their vulnerable moments and this was mine.

"Are you ok?" she understood something was seriously wrong.

"Can you come to me, please? I need you," I pleaded.

"Yes of course, I will come baby. But what happened?"

"I am not in a position to talk. I feel choked. Please come."

"I will be there within four hours. Don't go out anywhere. I will keep calling you every fifteen minutes to check on you. Don't worry," she consoled me.

She then called Simmi and apparently gave her instructions to keep an eye on me and take care of me until she arrived because I could sense that in Simmi's behaviour. To leave her daughter and parents, and rush to me immediately just because I said I needed her, spoke volumes about my importance in her life and her feelings for me. Actions speak louder than words and her actions spoke through the bullhorn that I was her priority.

She reached in a little over four hours. She entered the house in an obvious sense of urgency and kissed Rey on her way to the balcony, where I lay like dead meat. As soon as she came to me, I gathered all my strength to get up and hug her tight, without thinking what Simmi and Rey would think. Getting a dose of her physical presence and touch felt like a man getting his first bite of food after a week of hunger-strike.

"Hey, are you alright?" she asked.

"I don't think so," I replied.

"Everything is fine, Abby. I am here now, don't worry," she said.

"Sit down and breathe first. We will talk later," she said when she noticed my laboured breathing and asked Simmi to bring me a glass of water.

"I was kidnapped today morning at Mahesh's behest, when I was returning from my walk," I spoke up.

"Kidnapped!" she gasped.

"Shhh... I don't want Rey to know. Yes, kidnapped," I repeated.

"Let's inform the police at once," she murmured.

"No use doing that. The police are hand-in-glove with him."

"How can you say that?"

"The people who abducted me were cops."

"What?" she was astounded.

"But why did they abduct you? To browbeat you into withdrawing the case?" she continued.

"Yes, or they would harm those close to me."

"This is what you were waiting for, right? I have been telling you to back off, but you have been inexorable," Shalini was upset.

"I am too defenseless right now for you to bash me for it."

"Sorry! Did they get physical with you?"

"None of that matters against what Mahesh alleged about Myra," I said and enlightened her on everything Mahesh had told me.

"Don't trust Mahesh, it could well be his strategy to divert the case yet again. From what I know about Myra through you, she was as perfect as a woman can ever be. Nobody knew her better than you. Do you think she could have any such secret?"

"I don't think so, but there is no smoke without fire. There is definitely something about Myra that I am unaware of and I won't find peace till I get to the bottom of it."

"Let's not do anything in haste that we might have to regret later. We will discuss and figure out what to do next. But first things first, calm yourself down," Shalini tried to calm me down.

It took me a couple of more hours to crawl out of my anxiety and while I was at it, she was constantly by my side. She fed me like a baby and caressed my forehead to help sleep overpower me for about half an hour.

I insisted her to stay the night and she agreed, not just for that night, but for a couple more because she wouldn't leave me alone till she was convinced I was fine and in control. I couldn't help falling for her care, a care rooted in the fact that she loved me more than anyone else in her life.

As she put Rey to sleep after dinner, I waited impatiently for her in the balcony under the freshly sprouted stars in the night sky. Amazed by the view of the skyline at night and how the brightly lit buildings filled the horizon, I wondered when my dark life would be similarly lit with happy moments. The way my life had tied itself into umpteen number of knots, it seemed impossible to untie it. There was just one glimmer of hope that I was clung to, Shalini.

"Hey, how are you feeling now?" Shalini came to my side and slipped her hand under mine. Our fingers automatically intertwined.

"Better but still restless," I replied, my voice ragged.

"I can understand. Did you think about the way forward?"

"I want to know the truth about Myra. Though I trust her completely, it's a test of our love and I want proofs to rip Mahesh's allegations apart."

"That brings me to a suggestion," she said looking at me.

"What?"

"I believe our conclusions should be based on an objective investigation and not on our beliefs. I feel you might be biased in finding proofs or the lack of it because of your love and trust on Myra. And if you do come across any evidence of something objectionable against her, it might get to you, making it difficult for you to maintain your sanity because of your intense feelings for her. If you are really interested in knowing the truth, let me deep-dive and unearth the facts with a neutral mind. But that is only if you trust me," she suggested.

"Of course, I trust you and I get your point. Thanks for offering to do this."

"Anything for you, Abby. I am sure Myra will come out clean."

"I hope so! What do you think Myra could be hiding, if there is any truth to what Mahesh claimed?"

"I can't say for sure, but just thinking out aloud. She could be having an extramarital affair. It would make things embarrassing for a married woman if the affair came to light."

"Myra was very committed to our relationship and she was very possessive about me. She wouldn't get into an affair with some other man," I reasoned with her.

"When a woman is possessive about her man, it does not necessarily imply that she herself would not get into any relationship outside marriage. It just means that she would not like her husband to get into another relationship so that she gets his undivided attention. It does not stop her from seeking attention from other men or getting involved with one," she explained to me.

"What crap are you talking?"

"It's like logical reasoning. And I am playing devil's advocate here, remember?"

"I get it. When she knew I loved her so much, why would she go out seeking love from somebody else?"

"It can happen in a marriage over a period of time, Abby. It is not a question of whether or not the husband actually loves his wife. It is about the perception that the wife has, of whether the husband loves her or not. The same is true if we switch the genders."

"Go on."

"Was there any period when she thought you didn't love her like before or you had changed for the worse?" she further asked.

"Yes, there was. I had told you about it. It was after Rey was born and she was apparently in her postpartum depression."

"Did she start paying extra attention to herself to look better around the same time your relationship hit a low? It could be like going to the gym regularly, frequent parlour visits, dressing up hot to draw male gaze, etc."

"She always dressed well. However, she had started taking kickboxing classes and going on daily brisk walks in the society even at 1 a.m. in the night, which she never used to do earlier. But that was probably because she had to lose weight and gain some confidence," I told her.

"Losing weight could also be for someone else, not ruling out the feel-good effect it has on oneself. Did she go out often, including partying until late night with any of her ex-boyfriends, if any, or some new guy she must have met online?"

"She used to go out quite frequently until she got pregnant the second time. I am not aware of all the people she went out with, but I know for sure that she did go out with Vikrant, her ex-boyfriend, quite a few times."

"And you never stopped or questioned her?" Shalini asked me.

"Why would I? It was her life and she was free to do anything she wanted to."

"Well, she didn't think the same about you doing whatever you wanted to. Anyway, have you met Vikrant?"

"I had first met him years ago when Myra had invited him to our anniversary party. Remember, I had told you about him when you had asked me after seeing our photo together on Facebook?"

"Oh yeah, I do. When did you last meet him?"

"I think a few months before Myra passed away. But he is a great guy and we were very good friends. I trust him."

"Great guys have greater secrets. Tell me one thing, was she always on the phone, chatting with or calling people?"

"Always, so much so that her nickname was *Phone Kumari.*"

"Did you check her phone to find out who she talked to or chatted with?"

"No, that would have been invasion of privacy. Also, she had her phone locked with a passcode I didn't know."

"What? She was your wife, Abby."

"Yeah, right! She was my wife, not my slave. She was free to do what she wanted to and was also not obligated to share her passcode with me."

"Ah! Was she abnormally possessive about her phone?"

"Yes, kind of."

"And still, you never bothered to check her phone?" Shalini was surprised at my words.

"I trusted her. There was no reason not to."

"Unbelievable! Let me remind you, this isn't *Satyuga.* I wish we had her phone, but it must be with the police as the case hasn't closed yet. She had an iPhone?"

"No, an Android one."

"By any chance, do you have the back-up of it on Google drive?"

"It might be on Myra's Google account but I don't have the password for that either," I said.

"Thought as much. I don't think we will be able to crack anything without the phone. That is the only remote control to the light that will illuminate her secrets, if there are any."

"Don't you think if her phone had any such information, the police would have brought it to light already? They must have checked the phone for sure."

"You think our police works properly? If it did, Mahesh would have been behind bars by now. The phone must be lying uselessly in some police locker."

"Yeah, I second that. Let's go ahead with whatever we have."

"No other option. Which mobile operator did you guys use?"

"Airtel. Both our numbers were in my name."

"So, we can get her mobile bills from the Airtel store, or...," Shalini was thinking.

"Or?"

"I am guessing the registered email id was yours for both the numbers."

"Yes, I can share the login credentials of that email account with you."

"Great, so I can download all of Myra's e-bills. Any other information you have that might be useful?"

"Yes, she went to Goa once with her school friends, all girls. It was a combination of a solo-trip and an all-girls' trip."

"Can you elaborate on that?"

"She went to Goa for a total of five days, out of which she was alone there for the first two days as she wanted an experience of a solo-trip. Her friends joined her on the third day," I told her.

"Interesting. Where did she stay?"

"Homotel, Candolim."

"Thanks, I will let you know if I find anything," she said as she made notes like a diligent detective.

"But don't you think we are looking unilaterally at the extramarital angle only? Why couldn't it be some other angle too?" I wasn't ready to believe that Myra could have an affair.

"I don't think so, unless she was a spy or something which she definitely wasn't," she brushed off my question as frivolous.

"Something infelicitous could have happened during one of her night-outs with some friend or a friend of friend or a complete stranger who could have befriended her online or at some nightclub. That could be another possibility," I came up with a valid scenario.

"Agreed... So, let's start with the top of the head possibility and do a course-correction as we move ahead, if it is required."

"Fair enough. You would have done well as a detective. You didn't play the devil's advocate, you played the Satan himself," I was impressed with her interrogation that was quite rigorous, given that it was impromptu.

"Listen, we can decide on not digging up Myra's past and I am absolutely fine with it. In fact, I suggest we don't investigate this. Ignorance is bliss; we can let your relationship with her be hunky-dory and an epitome of true love for you, me and everyone who knows you. I am sure Mahesh is bluffing but deep down, I am apprehensive of going ahead with this because just in case we do stumble upon something against Myra, your faith in true love will take an irreparable hit. You might never believe in love again, neither would the world. That would affect me too, because I am seeing my future with you and I would never want to jeopardize it. Maybe, we should just let it be and forget about it," she warned.

"I want to face it, whatever it is. My relationship with Myra, good or bad, will not decide my relationship with you," I was ready, at least I thought so.

"Ok, I will do it for you."

"Thanks!"

"Coming back to the investigation, phone bills alone will not be enough for a foolproof look-into. We need to get our hands on her phone and we can't until the case is on. What have you thought about withdrawing the case?" she pondered and fired another question that was still open since my abduction and held the key to getting Myra's phone back.

"As much as I can think in my current mental condition, I should withdraw the case because Mahesh has now started acting on his threats and I don't want my loved ones harmed," I told her.

"I think likewise. But why has he started executing his threats now?" she was intrigued.

"It is because of the political pressure as the elections are around the corner. Also, it is now that the court has asked for proofs against him."

"I was always in favour of you taking the hopeless case back. If you are sure about it, it is better to go ahead tomorrow itself rather than delay and confront another mishap. It will also help us in getting our hands on Myra's phone sooner."

"I agree, but getting her phone back might take some time. You know how slow things move here."

"Not if Mahesh Prajapati is standing in the dock. As soon as he gets to know about you kickstarting the withdrawal of the case, which he is eagerly waiting for, things will move lightning fast to close everything. So, you can try your luck by going to the Police Station in a couple of days and asking for the phone," Shalini said.

"Can you, please? I want to stay away from Myra's phone. It has taken a lot out of me emotionally to get out of the abysmal pit of depression due to her death. I dread her phone might act as an emotional blackhole that would engulf me back into darkness."

"Fine, I will do it. Just give me an authorizing letter for the same."

"Sure!"

I had to admit, she was the panacea for all my problems and if there ever existed a deserving woman apart from Myra I would fight the world to marry, it was her.

"Once you withdraw the case and we are done with our investigation, start life afresh. Start writing or maybe, join a job for some time. You will meet new people and that will do you good. You can't be sitting idle doing nothing professionally," she suggested.

"Not yet, I need to work on Plan B," I had other plans.

"Plan B?"

"Yes, Plan B, to take control of things in my own hands and punish Mahesh."

"Oh god! Abby, don't ruin your life and along with it, everyone else's. Sorry to say, but this isn't a movie. The end of it might not be worth it and it will definitely screw us all."

"I know that Shalini, but I will stand by my *Law of Revenge*," I plainly told her.

"What is this shitty law of yours?"

"*Revenge MUST be extracted in equal measure, no matter what.*"

"So, you are telling me indirectly that you are going to kill Mahesh?" Shalini was getting furious.

"Not indirectly, I am telling it to you directly. I will deprive him of his life."

"What rubbish?" she was annoyed.

"I am serious."

"And how exactly are you thinking to pull your plan off?"

"There is no plan yet, but the end goal is clear."

"You have got to be kidding me! Clearly, that's your illogical and impractical anger talking, not you. We will talk about this when you get back to your senses. Let's first action on withdrawing the case tomorrow itself."

"I hate to say it, but yes, I will set things rolling tomorrow to quit the case, like a coward."

"That is not being coward, Abby. Very often, there are things that are beyond our control and we need to be practical. You are doing just that and I hope you think on similar lines to scrap your Plan B, too."

"I don't want to be unfair to Myra's love. I hope you understand where I am coming from," I told her.

"If I don't understand, who will? I love you and I will be with you in whatever you decide and do," she sealed our discussion with a warm hug and a peck on my lips.

Shalini returned to Pune the next day while I asked my attorney to file an application for withdrawal of the case citing my deteriorating health condition, with supporting medical reports to be submitted in the coming days. I purposely asked him to inform Mahesh's counsel about the same, not only for obvious reasons of safety, but also for delegating my work of sourcing the forged medical documents to Mahesh, which was effortlessly taken care of.

Shalini was right. The case was miraculously and briskly closed for good, within a week of my application, without a penny of bribe, which proved the hypothesis that a large part of the judicial system too, apparently wagged its tail in front of these political behemoths.

Shalini got Myra's phone from the police when she visited Mumbai for a couple of days right after the case officially closed. When she came back from the Police Station with the phone after vanishing from the house for close to eight hours, she was terribly miffed.

"Her phone is locked for eternity because it is locked with her Face ID. I took the phone to the service centre, but they failed to unlock it. They said it could erase all the data on the phone if they tried to do it," she was dejected.

"Wait a minute," I gave her my phone with Myra's photo on it and asked her to flash it in front of Myra's phone. I heard a sharp blip of the phone unlocking, bringing a winning smile on her face.

"That was smart," she complimented.

"I didn't know there were Face ID phones in 2015. I thought they came in 2017 for the first time," she further inquired out of curiosity.

"Face ID came on iPhones in 2017. Google had launched this feature on Android phones way back in 2011, as far as I remember. But these phones had a bug, at least until 2015, due to which they could be unlocked using photos," I enlightened her.

Shalini left for Pune with Myra's phone. She promised she would be back next week with her findings after analyzing all the information she had at her disposal. That one week was the longest ever in my life. Throughout the week, I kept myself busy with Rey. From what I could make out from our late-night video calls that happened after she got free from her office and Sia, her room was littered with printouts; printouts that were apparently Myra's chats with different people, her mobile phone bills and probably some random documents.

Though I experienced several bouts of strong urges to get involved in Shalini's scrutiny of my love, I never asked her any question to avoid influencing her judgement and she never told me anything she discovered during the week. But her eyes were conspicuous in giving away an insinuation that things were far worse than what either of us had imagined.

CHAPTER 10

Location: Mumbai
Time: September 2019

Closing the case airlifted a huge burden off my head, but the same mammoth load now fell on my heart to design and execute an expectedly arduous, dangerous and intensive Plan B to seek revenge and uphold my *Law of Revenge*. I was always a control freak and the way things had gone to throw the entire control of executing Mahesh in my hands, it was nonetheless some respite from being dependent on unscrupulous others for justice.

When I informed my parents about chucking the case, they said they had wanted me to move on, but were hesitant to suggest the same, fearing my reaction. They were obviously relieved, having no inkling of my intention to literally go for the kill.

Shalini visited me in Mumbai to present the findings of her weeklong investigation in person.

"Let's sit after dinner tonight," Shalini said while we were having dinner.

"Are you done with the probe?" I asked.

"Yes."

"Good news or bad?" I was skeptical.

"It is good if you are an optimist, and bad if you are otherwise. Let's discuss after Rey's asleep."

Her reply made me jittery. It was clear, she had found proof of Myra's betrayal. Imagine going to school to collect your report card, knowing you have failed your examination. Waiting for Shalini's revelation of my relationship's report card was similar and I was waiting for the inevitable.

The two hours that we took to finally settle down at our usual place of conversation in the balcony, gave my overthinking and anxiety ample time to invite their best friend, migraine to gatecrash our discussion.

"Abby, if you want, we can still skip the discussion on what I found about Myra. We can conveniently avoid it," Shalini proposed.

"Save me your advice and cut straight to the findings," I could not wait any longer.

"As you wish, but you may not like what you hear. Embrace for impact," she warned.

"Don't worry about it," I was irritated.

"Her call records show multiple calls every day on select numbers. The list of such numbers include numbers of your mom, her parents, you and someone named Stuti."

"Stuti is her school friend and she stays in Bengaluru," I gave her the missing information.

"There are two people named Stuti in her contact list, Stuti Bangal and Stuti New. The school friend you are talking about is Stuti Bangal, but the Stuti I am talking about is the latter one."

"Stuti New must be a new number of the same Stuti. I know her very well."

"I wish that was true. I ran a check of the number on Truecaller and guess whose name showed up, Vikrant's!"

"Give me the number, let me check," I reconfirmed her claim in my phone's contacts; she was right.

"This means they were close and something was definitely brewing between them," she put forward her hypothesis.

"This is not conclusive. They might be good friends like we were when Myra was there," I disagreed.

"Talking to a guy who was her ex-boyfriend and that too for an average of over an hour every day falls beyond the gamut of good friends. Note that the incoming calls from Vikrant are not reflected in the bills and hence, not included in the talk-time I am reporting," she handed me the mobile bills with the highlighted entries of calls to Vikrant.

"Gosh!" I was flabbergasted seeing the highlighted entries in the dozen pages I browsed through.

"I will still give her the benefit of doubt. Her talking to anyone, including Vikrant was fine. I am sure it was nothing more than an innocuous friendship and those calls were just to vent out her feelings," I supported Myra.

"Don't let your love cloud your thinking. Why would she save Vikrant's number in Stuti's name? She was using precaution, no pun intended."

"Did you find any objectionable chat history between the two?" I was in dilemma by now.

"Her WhatsApp chats to Stuti New *aka* Vikrant, seem deleted for the most part. I could only find normal messages of wishing each other on various festivals and of course, on

Valentine's Day. It is hard to believe that one would chat so infrequently with a person who she talked daily to. At more than a couple of places, I found the reply to some question but the question itself was missing, confirming that the chat was deleted in patches. It's like, you don't send a 'Yes' after wishing 'Happy Valentine's Day' to each other, right? She was human and must have missed deleting them. It is obvious, deleting chats was a safety measure to keep their affair discreet."

"Oh, she must be grouching about me and that's ok. You really had me nervous with the way you cautioned me to embrace myself for the impact."

"The turbulence has just started," she said handing me printouts of some more documents.

As I sifted through the printouts, the panic sweat that had just evaporated from my forehead, condensed and fell back in its place. Those documents were invoices from Homotel, Goa.

"What are these?" I asked clutching the papers feebly.

"You could call them third confirmatory set of proofs," she said as I kept staring at her blankly.

"Myra had gone to Goa in first week of June 2015?" she continued.

"Yes, right after I had submitted the proposal of my novel to a publisher in May end. She had been looking after Rey single-handedly since February to allow me the time to wrap up my novel so that it could be out by her birthday in October. She wanted the novel as her birthday gift. Once I submitted the proposal, she asked to go on a solo trip to Goa that would turn into an all-girls' trip after two days."

"Turns out that solo trip of hers was a *dolo* trip with Vikrant. Have a look at the hotel bills of both."

"I don't understand what's written here," I was losing my mind and with it, my ability to comprehend.

She took the bills from my trembling hands and walked me through them. Vikrant stayed in the same hotel as Myra but in a different room for the first two days of her trip. Having walked through the earlier two proofs, a 'different' room didn't mean anything and was not a point to raise to defend Myra's virtue that was on sale here.

"I have something more to show you," she held my hand in hers with pity in her eyes.

"I found this in the 'Files' folder of her phone. It is the blood test report confirming her second pregnancy," she presented her fourth set of evidence and it was the final nail in the coffin.

"When did you come to know about her second pregnancy?" she asked.

"On our court marriage anniversary, July 19," I remembered the exact date when she had surprised me with the news.

"Going by what you had told me that time, it was a strip test. So, the confirmatory blood test was done after July 19. Am I correct?" she wanted to confirm.

"Yes, it was the very next day," I was clueless as to how the report was related to Vikrant or maybe, I wanted to remain so.

"Somebody else knew about the pregnancy before you did and it was Vikrant. This report's date is July 14. If you observe, the phone number mentioned on the report is Vikrant's which means she went for the blood test with him. I believe, Myra was not carrying your child; it was Vikrant's, and in all likelihood, the seed of it was sown in those two days of their Goa honeymoon."

Her back-to-back presentation of proofs without giving me the time and space to process things felt like powerful, emotional blows raining down on me, not giving me a chance to get back up and fight, the last one being the invincible knockout punch.

I felt my heart crack from within, causing a shooting pain in my chest. Despite the airiness of the balcony, I was feeling breathless. Unable to hold on to my eyelids any longer, the tears fell off. My tottering legs followed suit to let go of my body as I took support of the glass balustrade to slowly come down on my knees and eventually sit on the floor feeling emasculated, helpless and pitiable. Shalini kneeled down and buried my head in her chest as my cracked heart shattered to bits, sending pangs of pain through my body.

"Why did she do this to me Shalini? I loved her so much; I didn't deserve this. I sacrificed everything for her – my dreams, my profession, my company... everything. I was even ready to take up a job and become a slave at some corporate prison for her happiness. And this is what I got in return," the silent falling of tears exploded into inconsolable bawling.

"I am so sorry, Abby. We need to understand that nobody in this world is god. People make mistakes and Myra was no exception. She must have had her reasons," she tried to pacify me as I felt drops of tears trickle to my scalp, from her eyes that couldn't see me in such a pathetic state.

"What reasons, Shalini? Her happiness meant everything to me. She just had to tell me once that she wanted to be with Vikrant and I would have let her go, even if that meant a lifetime of sorrow for me. I treated her like a princess and literally fought with everyone who hurt her in any way, but she treated me like a drudge.

"Four years since her death and I was still ready to risk my life to go after Mahesh. And what did she do? She insulted my love, splintering its innocence and purity into pieces that I will never be able to assemble back for anyone."

"No, no, no Abby, don't say this."

"True love does not exist. It is a fact, no matter how much we lie to ourselves. I will never love anyone for the rest of my life. Screw these romance novels and movies that propagate the idea of true love just to sell their stories and make money out of them while we, the common people, fall into their trap and end up overlooking the fine line that exists between their fantasies and our reality. The result of it? Well, I am experiencing it first-hand."

"I should have misrepresented information and not told you the truth," Shalini was remorseful.

"Thank you for deciding against it. I feel like such an idiot. I was slogging my ass for her while she was having an emotional and sexual carnival behind my back. She accused me of having an affair with you when she was the one who was having one and I could not even sniff it, thanks to my blind faith in her. Now I get it; since she had the mindset of having an extramarital affair, she suspected the same about me, just like a thief thinks everyone else is a thief. Imagine her audacity, that promiscuous woman was going to give birth to someone else's child and like the biggest dullard in the universe, I was over the moon thinking it was mine. I fucking howled in pain for that baby when the doctors couldn't save it. And Vikrant, he was like a brother. I always trusted him and respected him for who he was. How the hell did he dare to wheedle his way into Myra's life and pee on mine?" I was a ball of embarrassment, frustration and anger, aware of the fact that the revelation would serve as a daily kick in the balls for the rest of my life.

"Tell me this is all a nightmare and wake me out of it. Please Shalini," my last words faded into a whisper.

"I don't know how to calm you down, Abby. I wish I had the answers to your questions. Whatever Myra did and for whatever reasons, it is in the past. From what I know and what I have experienced being with you, you have been the best husband a woman could ever ask for, and if Myra chose to betray a man like you, she should be the one feeling miserable, not you. She got her payback by losing you. However, let's not stoop so low as to vilify her or think bad about her since she is no more. There is no point. She must have had her reasons that might have seemed right to her. She was the love of your life at some point in time and let's respect her for that. Going by what you had told me, she was your wife and not your slave. She had the freedom to make her own choices in life and she did, albeit with a horrendous payback. The way I see it, unearthing her affair has set you free from the compulsion of extracting a life-threatening revenge and from the guilt of her death you have been carrying on your shoulders for so long. You can't change the past, but you certainly can make your future the happiest part of your life; that's what is in your control. It is time to offload Myra's baggage and get up to speed in life."

"Yeah, you are right; I will move on. I will erase Myra from my life. I will not crumble under her fall from grace and grovel in the dust of her immorality," I mustered all my strength to get back up on my feet.

"For four years, I have been mourning her death, but tonight, I will celebrate," I went to my bar table to get us two glasses and a bottle of wine.

"Abby, are you ok? You are scaring me," Shalini was baffled.

"I am fine, in fact, more than fine," I said pouring the drink into our glasses.

"Cheers to the fool becoming enlightened!" I gulped the wine.

It didn't take us long to get drunk and our inebriated states led us to our favourite room to have some 'quality time'. The feelings for Myra did not shackle me this time while making love to Shalini; they liberated me instead. I felt light and free in the truest sense of the words. There was no guilt, none at all, as I patiently made love to her without worrying about anything or anyone, living or dead. There was no fear of Myra's ghost. In fact, I wanted it to visit me that night for real and cower behind the same chair she had sat on last time, to witness me getting thoroughly consumed in our unrestricted display of love. It was as if that passionate union with Shalini was my innovative technique of doing planchette to call her spirit and make her suffer.

"I love you, Abby. It feels so good to have you back in my life," Shalini breathed.

"I feel likewise. Thank you for coming back into my life and saving me. The truth would have never come out if it weren't for you. I would have gone for Plan B, instead of digging up Myra's past so diligently," I felt blessed.

"Does that mean Plan B is dropped?"

"Unquestionably! My revenge was fueled by my love for Myra. When that love is no longer there, there can't be revenge."

"Thank god!" there was an unspeakable relief in her tone.

"That filthy, little bitch made a fool out of me. I was so naïve. I never asked her any intruding questions on her whereabouts and friends, and that slut misused the freedom I gave her while strangling mine. She will rot in hell," I gnashed my teeth as anger washed over me.

"There were also some personal notes she maintained on her phone, just in case you want to skim through them."

"Whatever I have seen is enough for this life; I don't want to see anything more on it. In scientific experiments during college, three concurrent readings were enough to draw conclusions. I have already seen four solid proofs consistent with each other. There is no need for the fifth one. I am done with her and her memories," I forced Myra's memories away as they tried to trespass my mind.

"It will take some time, but get rid of all the negative thoughts and start life afresh. Take a step back, join a job for some time and then get back to writing. And promise me, your next novel will be on our love story," Shalini advised.

"I am not too keen on joining any company, but since you are asking me to, I will ruminate on it."

Completely drained of our energy by the varied turn of events that night, ending with a lengthy workout on the bed, she dozed off, but sleep eluded me. For her, Myra's chapter was closed, but for me, a new chapter had unknowingly flung open.

CHAPTER 11

Location: Mumbai
Time: September 2019 - October 2019

Shalini stayed with us for one more day and left for Pune to be with Sia, leaving me with a feeling of loneliness and a lot of heartache. It was quite unusual for me to feel something so strongly for anyone after Myra. On probing deeper into my heart to ascertain the reason, I discovered that my love for her had become more deep-rooted than ever before. She had plunged deeper into my heart with the things she had done for me in the last few years, which were way beyond the confines of my expectations from her.

There was a sense of relief and calm, but it was intermittently and constantly being punctured by an inexplicable feeling of some unfinished business. With the compunction of betraying Myra vaporizing into thin air after last night's revelations, I wanted to touch base with the inner Abby to know why I still wasn't feeling completely unfettered.

"*Something is bothering me and I am not able to decipher it. Is there something pending?*" I asked inner Abby.

"*What's vexing you is another betrayal; betrayal from a friend who you considered as your brother,*" inner Abby was bang on in locating the exact reason of my botheration just like an orthopedist or a dentist magically pin-points the exact location of pain.

"*Yeah, I felt the strain in my head as soon as you struck that chord. I am not letting that smut get away with what he did. It isn't about Myra's revenge, it's about mine this time. That scumbag betrayed me and deserves a befitting reprisal. I need you to tell me what to do, preferably without breaching the legal barriers.*"

"Apply your *Law of Revenge. What he did to you, you should do to him. It's like an eye for an eye and a fuck for a fuck. He is a good-looking guy and must surely have a love interest. Find that someone and bonk her,*" I was impressed how clear inner Abby's thinking was, every single time.

"*How will I do that? Can you help me plan for it?*" I asked.

"*Why don't you ask Shalini? You have been following her suggestions and looks like it has augured well for you,*" inner Abby remarked sarcastically.

"*I don't want her to know about it. She wants me to move on in life and will disapprove of me going after anyone to avenge myself. More importantly, she loves me to bits and will obviously never agree to me sleeping with another girl. I can't ask her,*" I reasoned, failing to get inner Abby's sarcasm.

"*Now can you plan for me? How do I find Vikrant's girlfriend and how do I get her?*" I continued.

"*In today's times, social media is the king and you will find every information you are looking for on it, be it about anyone – from celebrities to common people. Stalking his social media profiles will give you the lead about his girl. If there isn't any, he might be gay and you might have to sleep with a guy if you wish to stand by your law.*"

"Oh! With all due respect to people who have whatever type of sexual preferences, I will backtrack in that case. In the course of fucking his life and making him suffer, I don't want to fuck a guy, literally."

"He dated Myra and apparently impregnated her. Obviously, he is straight. Shalini appears to have rusted your brain."

"Leave Shalini out of this, please. I love her."

"So, you find his love interest and meet her like a stranger, without telling her that you know Vikrant. Woo her and then, fuck her."

"With the objective of inseminating her, and then sneak out from her life. Cool!"

"But on second thought, that's not you, Abby. You should refrain from going ahead with this. Maybe, just let the girl know what Vikrant did and let her do the rest. If you hoodwink her into sleeping with you and just in case knock her up, you will be making her suffer unnecessarily for no mistake of hers. I think that will be too heartless of you; she didn't hurt you, Vikrant did," the argument continued.

"So, should I fuck and impregnate Vikrant? Come on, she will be counted as collateral damage! Now, stop being a sentimental fool; no one's god here, including me. I need my revenge."

It didn't take much of my time to figure out Vikrant's lady love *aka* his wife. Her name was Monali Patil and they had been married for the last three years, with no kids. The fact that Monali was Vikrant's wife and not his girlfriend would turn the tables perfectly between him and me. Besides that, it would save me from setting out on a future guilt trip of impregnating – in case the plan was successful – an innocent girlfriend (as against wife), who would have been subsequently shunned by Vikrant to fend for herself when he found out about it. For a wife, the husband would not even get a hint of an outsider knocking his wife up, just like it had happened for me. In all probability, the wife would be able to carry on with her husband, albeit with her own guilt of cheating on him.

Monali's life was an open book on her Instagram profile that was thankfully not private. From her photos, she looked pretty attractive, the kind of girl guys would be lusting after. She seemed quite social and bubbly, who loved meeting people and partying, as evident from her posts. She was a self-proclaimed traveller, adventurer, teacher and an avid reader, going by what was explicitly mentioned in her Instagram *bio.*

Meeting her randomly at a night club or a coffee shop was going to be highly dependent on my luck, whose track record wasn't that great. Being at the same place as her at the same time would mean I would have to proactively check her Instagram story, figure out which place she was at and rush to that spot, followed by another tedious task of finding an opportune moment to approach and impress her. Another option was messaging her directly on Instagram and asking her to meet, an option too cheap and unreliable. Both options required me to be a Tom Cruise or a Ranbir Kapoor to make her drool over me and instantly fall in my trap. Unfortunately, I was not that good looking a guy a girl would crush over. So, both the options were ruled out.

I was presentable in looks and it wasn't something I could bank on completely. However, I did have intelligence and an amiable nature that had a history of attracting the opposite sex far better than my appearance, with a much higher success rate. So rather than a brief encounter, I needed an extended period with her at some place to sweep her off her feet to an extent that she would cheat on her husband.

Another session of bouncing off ideas with the inner Abby led me to the perfect and a more practical option, her workplace. The plan was to first try and join the same company where she worked and then take the plan forward from there. Joining a job would also be in line with Shalini's wish and would keep any kind of suspicion from her at bay. To her, it would seem that I was moving on in accordance with her advice, but to me, it would be aligned with my goal of delivering payback to Vikrant. I would quit the job as soon as I would be done.

My plan was expected to take a few months and it would need me to be absent from Rey's life for most part of the weekdays due to office, which would mean his complete dependence on Simmi, who I did not completely trust, though Mahesh's episode was over. Since I didn't want his life and education to get affected in my absence, I decided to send him to Patna to stay with my parents and continue his schooling there, at least for the ongoing session. That would free me of his responsibility to focus on the task at hand and get it over with at the earliest.

Searching where Monali worked was a piece of cake. It didn't take much effort to look her up on LinkedIn and learn that she was working for an education technology start-up called Mentor.com as a manager in the Customer Experience vertical. She was based out of its Head Office in Powai, Mumbai.

Education sector was in my blood. I had previously set up an education company single-handedly and had written bestselling textbooks in Maths, Physics, Biology, etc., for IIT aspirants and students of Grades 1 to 12. Above all, I had degrees from the world's most reputed colleges to back me. I was confident I would get a job at Mentor, but what I was wavering about was whether or not I would be able to follow the routine life of an employee and take orders from someone above me in hierarchy, for the few months I would be a part of it. What if I snapped at something or someone and resigned?

I went through the stodgy task of revitalizing my resume and then applying to Mentor through multiple websites that didn't elicit any response from its Talent Acquisition team. At last, I came across a new job portal which was exclusively for candidates from the Ivy League colleges, mostly IITs and IIMs. It didn't disappoint and a recruiter called me to take things ahead.

Instead of the usual four rounds of face-to-face interviews for the Vice President position, I underwent six rounds spread over a week, making my wait longer, thus intensifying my anxiety. I was nervous because I really needed that job for the first and the most important phase of my plan to succeed. Luckily for me, Mentor needed me as well, and it was evident in each round of interview. Just that I didn't want to believe it till I had the offer letter in my hands.

I was told much later by the recruiter that the six rounds of interviews happened because my profile was pretty strong and the additional two interviewers just wanted to meet me. It was consistent with what the CEO, Zayn offered me in the last round.

"So Abby, what do you want to do at Mentor?" Zayn asked in a tone that was surprisingly heavy and loud for his built.

"Whatever Mentor wants me to do," I replied.

"All the interviewers wish to have you in their team. You have to choose now," Zayn offered.

"I believe Customer Experience is pretty new to the world and to Mentor, and is an extremely critical function. I can set that up for you if you want," my choice of vertical was driven by my personal interest in Monali, and not by my professional interest to further my career.

"Done. Head the Customer Experience for us, build it and scale it up," Zayn hammered his decision like a magistrate, oblivious to my hidden agenda.

CHAPTER 12

Location: Mumbai - Goa - Mahabaleshwar
Time: October 2019 - January 2020

Mom-Dad were happy on hearing the news of my next step in life, thinking I was moving on, and readily accepted Rey's responsibility. My joining date was a month later in November. So, I had ample time to shift Rey to Patna and settle him there.

Shalini too was thrilled when I told her about Mentor's offer, unaware of my ulterior motive. I told her that I would be occupied with getting used to the new life and might be irregular in calls or catch-ups with her at least for the initial couple of months, and she had no reasons to complain. It was what she had wanted me to do and she promised her unconditional support for it.

I was introduced to Monali (Mona) on the very first day. She looked much hotter in person than in her pictures. The first thing I noticed about her was her height. She was about 5 feet 6 inches tall, taller than any girl I had ever dated or had a brief encounter with. She resembled the Bollywood actress Sonali Bendre to a great extent, just that she was a little but desirably chubbier. Her sharp features with a fair complexion made her even more enticing, the brown-coloured hair and dark brown eyes adding to her aura. To tie this to my context, I wouldn't have to try too hard to make love to her. She was the perfect stimulus but was expected to be a tough nut to crack and I would probably need a bulldozer to sweep her off her feet.

She was going to be my direct reportee in a team that was barely a four-member one, with Mona and her three subordinates. That meant a lot of one-on-one interaction with her, that would be conducive to nurturing our short-term relationship. The only question was how willing she would be to cross her limits as a wife and my only consolation was - she was human and was therefore, cursed to commit mistakes.

It started with our statutory introduction to each other and licit exchange of phone numbers over coffee in the office cafeteria amidst prying eyes of people inundated with envy. She seemed pretty impressed with my profile and expressed her surprise at why I had joined Mentor. I had specifically noticed her eyes lit up when she searched me on Google and discovered I was a bestselling author in English fiction as well as education genres. That was my cue for throwing my first anchor deep into her heart and I immediately fetched a copy of my novel from my bag, signed it with a lovely message and gifted it to her on the spot. It was a gesture that instantly brought a wide smile to her face and started my pursuit of her on the right foot. She promised she would read it over the weekend and get back with her feedback.

She gave me a quick download of the work she had done in the new vertical that was still a bambino. She hadn't had much luck in the pilot projects she had undertaken due to her own limitations.

While Mona was reporting to me, I was reporting to Sarvesh, who was the COO. Sarvesh or Sarvo, as he was fondly called at Mentor, was a great guy in the sense that he was smart, efficient and cool. The best part, he became a good friend or rather, a brother from another mother, right from the word go. Along with Zayn, we decided on some key objectives for which I designed a couple of pilot projects and got things rolling at once, working closely with Mona. Zayn and Sarvo entrusted me with their faith and though I had my personal agenda in mind, I decided to work sincerely to ensure Mentor didn't suffer in any way because of it.

I met tens of people at Mentor in the first week itself, all of them very co-operative and as surprised as Mona about me joining Mentor because of my professional background. In reply, I gave them concocted but believable reasons of my passion to impact the education sector on a larger scale which was possible while working for a company like Mentor.

The first week was undeniably the toughest with teething troubles of adjusting to the mundane, tiring life and it felt like I had joined back school. Getting up early in the morning everyday was a pain in the neck. I remember calling Shalini every morning before entering my office building in the first week to tell her that I wanted to put down my papers, only to receive her lengthy lectures of wisdom. I wanted to quit and think of an alternative plan, but I hung around.

The bubble of my first week's fatigue popped when I received an Instagram notification on Sunday morning. Mona had followed me on Instagram and posted a photo of her reading my novel while sipping coffee. *A cup of coffee and an entertaining novel – all you need on a Sunday morning* – her caption read. I followed her back without wasting a second and reshared her post on my profile to acknowledge her tip-off that she had started reading.

When you are an author who has written a book with himself as the protagonist, it becomes convenient to create an image of yours in the minds of the readers about who you are as a person. It came as another big win the next day in office when she told me that she loved the novel so much that she finished it in one go, and ended up being infatuated with the protagonist.

"Your novel is a masterpiece. It is so engaging, I could not put it down," she complimented.

"Thanks, that's motivating," I replied.

"And I absolutely loved the protagonist. He is based on you, right?" she induced butterflies in my stomach.

"Yes, but only to an extent. I am not an ideal man like him," I was humble.

"That I will see," she had mischief in her eyes.

"I read in detail about you on Google and also checked your social media handles. I am sorry about your wife," she continued.

"Don't be. It's in the past and there is no point thinking about it," I didn't want to talk about Myra.

"Hmm... When is your next novel coming?" she asked excitedly.

"Looks like I will have to start working on it sooner than I had planned."

"Immediately sir, it is eagerly awaited. And yeah, my husband knows you and you know him too."

"Really? What's his name?" I feigned ignorance.

"Vikrant. He said he has met you. He knew your wife, they were building friends."

"Oh! You are Vikrant's wife? Of course, I have met him. Small world, eh?" I said controlling my exasperation.

"The three of us should catch up some time," she offered.

"Without a doubt, but let me settle in here first," I procrastinated the meet-up.

Mona mapped all of the protagonist's attributes onto me and that worked heavily in my favour. Two months of relentlessly working closely with each other, understanding one another in bits and pieces both personally and professionally, did the rest. I taught her things, I guided and motivated her when she was disheartened, I supported her and exuded immense care and empathy when she was not well or was going through her monthly curse; I did everything the best boss in the world would do, impressing her in the process. All my efforts flowed out of me genuinely and appeared to pay off, for she was smitten by me and her eyes gave it away every time we interacted.

As part of my strategy to draw her closer to me, I liked all her posts on Instagram in the dead of night. When you like someone's posts at that time, you send a signal that you were thinking of her in your loneliest hours. That thinking is tacitly understood as fantasizing and it usually hits all the right notes when you are trying to pursue someone. Another social media strategy was checking all her WhatsApp and Instagram stories without fail and beating all her contacts and followers to it to be among the first ones to do so. It apparently worked because she reciprocated by emulating my behaviour.

When I presented the results of our first pilot project in front of two dozen people from Mentor, including Zayn and Sarvo, I was greeted with an unexpected thumping of tables to applaud the incredible numbers we had clocked. I seized the opportunity and made the move to fix my last anchor in Mona's heart by giving her the entire credit of the project, though I had done most of the work.

"It was your work, Abby and you gave the credit to me. That is unfair," she told me after the presentation.

"You deserve it, Mona. You have been great!" I complimented her.

"This is the corporate world and people here steal the credit from others, not serve it on a silver platter like you did."

"I am different," I was looking straight into her eyes.

"Yeah, you are indeed, exactly like the protagonist of your novel."

"That's a big compliment. Thanks."

"Thanks to you. The gesture was flattering and I am touched. I am not just a fan of you as an author but also you as a person now."

The seed of seducing Mona that had already sprouted into a healthy sapling with my previous moves, had now started bearing flowers owing to my latest manoeuvre. I started planning to pollinate those flowers into fruits, the fruits of my sweet revenge. All I needed was a 'bee' and that bee came in the form of a maiden three-day off-site planned in Goa by Mentor in January.

While Mona took a flight to Goa and reached eight hours before me, I decided to hit the road. The lag between her and my arrivals was pre-planned to check if she missed me because I wanted to test the waters before diving in and hunting her down. I just had three days with me for the kill and I needed to be sure of her emotional proximity to me for her to take that leap of corruption and betrayal. Despite having friends from office around her, put up in the same hotel, she did miss me confirming that the distance between us had narrowed enough.

"Hey, what time is your flight? I am getting bored," she called when I was driving.

"I am about to reach Amboli. It should take another two hours," I replied.

"Amboli? Are you driving to Goa?" she was taken aback.

"Yeah, and it is so much fun. I can't tell you," I conveyed my thrill knowing her penchant for road trips.

"That's so mean of you. Why didn't you tell me? I love road trips and would have loved to join you," she sounded upset.

"Oh! I wasn't sure you would be comfortable with me alone for close to nine hours," I reasoned to gain more of her trust.

"If I can't be comfortable with you, I can't be comfortable with anyone in the world. Come on, Abby!"

"Now that I know, we can drive back together to Mumbai," I offered.

"Deal?" she confirmed.

"Deal!" I froze the plan.

Her Goa trips had always been boring, either because she had gone there with her in-laws or parents, or because the friends she went with were keener on enjoying the property than exploring the infamous nightlife. Throughout the three days we stayed there for, we sneaked out multiple times from everyone's radar and stole some lone moments together, during which I helped her tick out items from her checklist to break her Goa jinx.

Since both of us were sharing our rooms with different colleagues, I didn't really get an opportunity to execute the climax of our short and sweet story. The times we spent together, nonetheless, pushed me closer to my objective. We talked about our favourite books, the movies we enjoyed, our secrets and our dreams for the future. In our inebriated states under the dark sky lit with stars, she let out some office gossip.

"You have created quite a wave at Mentor for being the most well-dressed, handsome and perfumed guy at office, apart from being intelligent," she said.

"That's news and a delightful one at that. Who thinks that about me?"

"Don't exploit my booziness; I will not take names. Just know that you have quite an impression on some females at office. People can literally smell your presence at office."

"What about you?"

"Me? Since my insobriety has given me the license, let me confess. I have a crush on you. But like a decent one," she said.

"The feeling is mutual except that it's both decent and indecent from my side. You are a woman straight from my dreams," I said only to floor her with my art of flattery.

Her blushing to my comment downed all the red flags I had in my mind to go ahead. The only problem, I couldn't execute my plan in Goa because I didn't want anyone at Mentor to get a whiff of my intentions. I had to wait till we were on our way back and thankfully, the wait was not for long.

On our way back to Mumbai, I offered her a detour to Mahabaleshwar to have a day of tranquility among the scenic views, before returning to the grind in Mumbai. She agreed and the plan was on. She did not inform Vikrant about our detour to squash any chance of him playing spoilsport in her adventure due to his suspicion of any kind.

We reached Mahabaleshwar in the afternoon and booked two separate but connecting rooms at an upscale hotel with breathtaking views of the valley. After treating ourselves to a sumptuous lunch, I handed her the manuscript of my unpublished short story that I had written years ago. For an avid reader, that's an exclusive treat. It barely took her an hour to devour my manuscript. As she heaped praises on my writing, I was calculating my next stride, standing in our balcony and staring blankly at her beautiful face.

We went around Mahabaleshwar in the evening and returned to our retreat after dinner. I poured out scotch for us to kickstart our drinking session in the balcony. The plan was to make her so drunk that she would let her guard down and let me do her without the slightest of shilly-shallying.

After four hours of quaffing, the stage was set for the grand finale. She was neither in her senses anymore nor in control of her body. When I picked her up in my arms to take her to bed, she completely surrendered her body to me as if I was her guardian angel and she trusted me with it. Holding her beautiful, enticing body so close to mine ruptured all my control valves. Like a werewolf, I was quickly turning into a lustful and vindictive monster ready to breach all lines of morality.

I wanted to enjoy my moment of victory that wasn't far off now. I put Mona on the bed and ogled her desirable body. With her lifted knee-length, black skirt that had betrayed her to bare her thighs, she was indeed a feast I would cherish. As she turned to her side, I joined her on the bed from behind which stimulated her to subconsciously push her rear against my crotch, sending blood and adrenaline gushing to all parts of my body.

"Revenge must have never been so hot," I whispered to myself, ready to plunge into her.

CHAPTER 13

Location: Mahabaleshwar
Time: January 2020

As I kissed Mona on her cheek and turned her to supine position with her body facing up, my eyes fell on her innocent face that was a window to her inner beauty and purity. I could hear the inner Abby lending his voice-over to my gaze.

"*This is not you, Abby. Don't do it. She is innocent and has nothing to do with what Vikrant did to you. She was not even there in his life when all that happened,*" inner Abby's words reverberated in my mind.

"*Not the time to fuck with me right now, buddy,*" I was not ready to back off, on the verge of my ultimate retribution.

"*Not the time to fuck with her, either. Just because Vikrant did something he shouldn't have, you shouldn't do the same. You are Abby, not Vikrant. You have values, he didn't. You are officially in a relationship with Shalini. If you cross the line tonight, you might lose respect in your own eyes and it won't be worth it. Mona genuinely likes you and might as well agree to sleep with you, but she also trusts you blindly as a mentor and it is your responsibility to stop her from doing anything as criminal as sleeping outside her wedlock,*" inner Abby hit the nail on the head and convinced me to abort my mission.

The next morning, Mona woke up in my arms. So technically, I did sleep with her but we didn't do anything outrageous and had our virtues intact. I decided I would expose her to the truth and let destiny take its course.

"I want to tell you something," I distanced myself a little from her, my eyebrows twitched.

"Did we...," she wanted to confirm if we did anything nefarious the previous night.

"No, we are still strangers, sexually. You passed out and I also dozed off beside you," I answered pre-empting her question.

"Oh, ok," she let out a long breath. I wasn't sure if it was a sigh of relief or a sigh of disappointment. It didn't matter. What was wrong, was wrong and I wouldn't do it.

"I want to tell you something else, Mona. It's a confession."

"That you are crushing over me? I know that and the feeling is mutual."

"Not that either. I hate to admit this but our night together was a part of the plan I had put together a few months ago. So, every single thing – joining Mentor, choosing the same vertical as you, gifting you my novel, stalking you on Instagram late at nights, giving you credit for the work I did, etc., was a façade created to lure you into liking and trusting me. I played with your mind and your heart to lead you into this detour with me. All of this was done with the ultimate intent of knocking you up and I got that chance last night, but my conscience played spoilsport."

"I don't believe this. Why did you put so much effort and time just for a night of passion with me when you have female fans more beautiful than me, who would probably love to spend the night with you? As far as I know, you are one of the most decent guys I have ever met. You wouldn't do this unless it was for a valid reason. I am definitely missing something here. What is it, Abby? You can tell me."

"Thanks for understanding, Mona. The thing is, Myra and Vikrant weren't just building friends. They dated each other for a while."

"I know that; Vikrant had told me."

"Did he also tell you he was clandestinely dating her after Rey was born?"

"What?"

"Did he tell you Myra was pregnant with his child?"

"Wait, wait, wait...! I don't think that's true. He told me everything about every girl he dated before our marriage, including the extent of his intimacy with them."

"He obviously would not tell you he impregnated his married ex."

"From what I know about Vikrant, he would never do something like that. I get your point, but weren't you also like a brother to him?"

"Yes, and he broke my trust by sleeping around with my wife. Myra was five months pregnant with his child and I had no clue because I trusted them both. I needed revenge from him, a tit for a tat and that is why I planned to pay him back in equal measure by bonking you."

"Do you have any proof for me to confront Vikrant on it, because if there is any truth to it, I will need to finish your last night's unfinished business in addition to divorcing him?" Mona was straight-faced.

"I have multiple proofs, but unfortunately, I am not carrying them with me. I will hand them over to you when we reach Mumbai. I have call records, hotel bills of their stay together, pregnancy test report with Vikrant's phone number as the registered phone number, etc.

"Having said that, there is no unfinished business, Mona. Let's not lose the purity of our souls in the process of penalizing the impure ones. You are a beautiful person inside and out, and I would love to have you as my friend forever," I asked for her friendship.

"I will be a friend and a fan. You are a gem," she concurred and hugged me.

"And yes, we can resume our last night's action when both of us are not in any relationship," I joked to ease the seriousness of the situation.

"Yeah, why not."

Inner Abby was right; I would have repented if I had gone ahead with my plan. I felt proud of myself that I didn't stoop down to Vikrant's and Myra's levels. I did waste my last few months plotting and executing stuff that ended in absolutely nothing. But as per Abby's Third Law of Life, *Everything happens for the best* and Mona's chapter also happened for the best. I assumed that 'best' to be closure of all the pending chapters of my life to start afresh with Shalini. Driving back to Mumbai with Mona, I was happy and at utmost peace for the first time in a long, long time, unaware of the 'best' that destiny had in store for me.

CHAPTER 14

Location: Mumbai - Goa
Time: January 2020

Mentor's role in my life had ended and there was no point dragging it along to my next destination which I still had to figure out. So, I put down my papers. Zayn and Sarvo were understanding enough to waive off my notice period and relieve me before my birthday on 24 January, but asked me to return to Mentor anytime I felt like.

Mona was disheartened on learning about my departure from Mentor, but I told her we'd be in touch. I did not give her the proofs purposely and advised her not to question Vikrant on Myra and her pregnancy. What Vikrant had done was before she came into his life and so, it made no sense to ruin her marriage for it or be stressed about it as Myra also was no more.

Nobody at home dared to question my decision to quit Mentor, fearing my emotional recoil, but they were not pleased with it. I told Shalini and my parents that I didn't want to die a regular employee; I wanted to achieve much bigger things in life. Moreover, the job at Mentor wasn't allowing me the mental and physical bandwidth to pursue my passion of writing that I was now ready for.

It had been quite some time since I had met Shalini and Rey. Our conversations over the last few months had also not been regular due to Mona and Mentor. My birthday seemed like the perfect time to spend some time together.

I travelled to Patna to get Rey to Mumbai for a few days. I didn't shift him to Mumbai permanently because I didn't want to muddle the continuity of his ongoing academic session in Patna. By this time, Mom and Dad were aware about Shalini and our tacit understanding of spending the rest of our lives together as man and wife. They expressed the desire to meet her, but I told them it would happen only after we formally committed to each other and it was expected very, very soon.

Next on the cards was another road trip to Goa, picking up Shalini and Sia on the way from Pune, to celebrate my birthday. The trip was not just for Shalini and me to spend some quality time together, but also for Rey and Sia to start bonding as friends for a facile transition to siblings. The half an hour early morning stop at Pune was also utilized in meeting Shalini's parents, who already knew me by face from our Grade 12 days when Shalini and I used to go to the same coaching class for our engineering entrance examination preparation. From what I could infer from their demeanour, they knew about Shalini and my endearment, and seemed more than happy to see their daughter planning to settle down with me.

The trip was more enjoyable than tiring because Shalini sat beside me on the front passenger seat. We managed to steal some brief but electrifying moments of stealthy hand-holding like teenagers whenever both the kids dozed off in the rear. I had booked a suite at Taj Resort and Convention Centre this time for the spectacular views of the sea from our suite as well as the hotel's huge rooftop terrace that suited the most for what I wanted to do.

On the eve of my birthday, after we put the kids to bed, I took Shalini to the terrace. Against the backdrop of the majestic Arabian Sea and under the scintillating sky riddled with glittering stars smiling down on us, I went down on my knees with a remote control in my hands in place of a diamond ring. The ring instead, broke into the scene riding on a drone that flew in seconds later while Shalini was still wondering what was happening.

"Will you be my partner in crime?" I proposed.

"Forever and ever," she agreed with tears of joy and wrapped an Apple Watch around my wrist that she had got for me as my birthday gift.

We hugged and kissed. It was weird how the universe had conspired to bring us back together, reaffirming our faith in destiny. Everything indeed happened for the best with the double-crosser Myra, the backstabber Vikrant, the murderer Mahesh and the insolent Prashant helping themselves out of our lives for perpetuity, or so I thought. Shalini was ecstatic but I could sense her parachute of exultation punctured by fragments of anguish.

"Aren't you happy?" I asked as we sunk in the couch on the terrace.

"Of course, I am," she replied with a plastic smile.

"We are going to start a new life together and it is my right to know what is bothering my would-be wife."

"I cannot deny you that right, now. I have somewhat not been at peace."

"What happened? All good?"

"I don't know. There is that constant fear of imperilment. I don't feel safe."

"You don't feel safe? From who?"

"Mahesh Prajapati."

"But he is long gone from our lives. And he hasn't done anything deleterious ever since I withdrew the case."

"His brother has lost the election and subsequently been sacked from the position of State Chief of the political outfit he was once an integral part of," she informed.

"But he was going to lose the election anyway because of the negative buzz around everything he promised but didn't do."

"These people are like stray dogs who can turn around and bite back any moment. You never know, he could pass the buck to Mahesh, blaming him for the loss because of the bad PR the court case brought him and Mahesh in turn could attempt to vandalize our lives, catching us unawares."

"That is unlikely. Don't overthink."

"Unlikely doesn't mean impossible. We are rebooting our lives with Sia and Rey. It is my family now and I cannot take any chance with its safety. I will do whatever it takes to protect it," Shalini was worried.

"What's going on in your head, Shalini?"

"We should take out Mahesh."

"Take out as in?"

"Your Plan B, let's do it Abby," she suggested.

"This is beyond my belief. You were the one who advised me against it, and now you yourself are contemplating it?" I said, completely shocked.

"If we don't do it, we will never be in peace. Both our kids will live their lives laden with fear. As parents, we should not let anything jeopardize their safety. Moreover, he had hurt my Rey almost fatally. Such a person deserves a place in hell, doesn't he?"

"Yeah, he does, but I don't agree with your logic for going ahead with Plan B. It is more likely to end in a disaster for us, even if we manage to nail Mahesh, because we are not seasoned criminals and I am not willing to roll the dice with Rey, Sia and you. The risk is clearly not commensurate with the reward. Look, I know you are trying hard to be a good mother, but I am scared that one little wrong move from us could magically fuck our lives up."

"We are not on the same page, Abby and that means I will have to do it alone."

"Now, that's like threatening me and it never works. Let's sleep over it, Shalini. We should never take decisions when we are emotionally charged up with hatred, anger, depression, love, excitement or whatever. Let's chew over it and discuss later when we are calmer and have reached our respective homes, or we would end up wrecking our beautiful family trip for the juniors."

"I get your point and I am fine with it."

For the next four days in Goa, until 28 January, we clung to our resolution and didn't discuss anything about Plan B. Leaving our kids in the play area, we would often sneak out for our quality (read as passionate) times together. The trip was no less than an oasis in the desert of our lives and we enjoyed every minute of it until the night before we left from Goa, when I started feeling the impending stress. The pending decision of setting out for Plan B was knocking at the door of my mind again, this time due to Shalini.

Shalini, Rey and Sia were already asleep in the bedroom while I was turning sides on my bed in the living room of the suite, with my perennial girlfriend – migraine. I wanted to distract myself to alleviate my headache, but wherever I tried to venture my mind into, the same thought of Plan B crawled back into it, until Mona came to my rescue.

"Hey Abby, where have you been? We need to catch up," she messaged.

"Hey, how are you? I am in Goa right now with Shalini, Sia and Rey for my birthday," I replied.

"Oh yeah! I am so sorry, I forgot. Belated Happy Birthday."

"That's ok. Thank you."

"When are you back?" she asked.

"I will be back tomorrow night (29th). But I will be leaving for Patna on 30th to drop Rey there and will be back again in Mumbai on 31st. Let's meet on 1 Feb?"

"Cool, block your date with me. Come alone, I will see you at JW Marriott, Juhu at around 5 p.m.," she was eager to meet, probably planning for a night together at the hotel after a tiff with Vikrant; the thought itself was a stuff of forbidden pleasures that I would try not surrendering to.

I didn't continue chatting with her, for it would have made Shalini suspicious about our bond, had she woken up. If she dug deeper into Mona and me, I would have to blurt out what

I was up to for the last few months and that would have soured our reincarnated relationship.

Having no other alternative but to fall asleep, I downed a couple of vodka shots and that magically doped me to sleep.

CHAPTER 15

Location: Mumbai
Time: February 2020

The session with Mona was an emotionally charging one, to say the least. The heavy drinking that I did while we spent one of the most profound and intense evenings of my life, left me hung over not for a day, but for days.

Mona handed me Vikrant's phone bills that she had downloaded from his mailbox from the year 2015 when I had claimed Myra was pregnant with his child. She had sourced Myra's phone number from Vikrant's contact list and diligently checked for it in his call records only to discover that the average frequency of their calls was once every fortnight with an average talk-time of only a few minutes per call, far less than what Myra's phone bills showed. It was highly unlikely that Myra called Vikrant daily for more than an hour and Vikrant called her just once every fortnight, and that too only for a few minutes. Myra knew I never checked on who she talked to. So, she wouldn't advise Vikrant to not call her and that she would be the one who would call him, almost always. And this raised serious doubts in my mind.

Shalini was the one who had pulled out Myra's phone bills that showed daily touchpoints with Vikrant. This meant either Mona had doctored Vikrant's bills to prove his innocence or Shalini was up to something, and I desperately needed to get to the bottom of it.

Lost in another world after my encounter with Mona, I needed to buy some time from Shalini to think straight and run a crucial background check. So, I suggested her to allow me a week or two for the thought of Plan B to settle in. We did meet a couple of times, but I could not cozy up with her due to the turmoil in my head. I mostly remained pensive and ensured I didn't lock my eyes with her for too long, lest she would peep into my soul and know things I didn't want her to know.

The background check unearthed mindboggling facts which left me in complete disarray. I downloaded Myra's phone bills from my inbox myself, and matched them with the bills Shalini had produced. They were inconsistent with each other; Shalini had tinkered with the bills before handing them over to me.

The hotel bills were also sourced by Shalini. It was obvious, I had to run a check on their veracity too. I called the hotel, but the staff wasn't ready to share information about any guest, as per its policy. So, I flew down to Goa and met the General Manager of the hotel. Luckily for me, she was a woman who understood emotions better than a man. I didn't fake any story and told her the truth about why I wanted her to check if Vikrant stayed at the property at the same time as Myra. To make my pitch stronger, I added that it wasn't a breach of their policy because I needed the answer in a 'yes' or a 'no' to a pointed question. The pitch worked and I got my answer; it was a clear-cut no.

Next up was verifying the pregnancy report which was also procured by my love, Shalini. The clinic that had apparently issued the report dismissed Myra's pregnancy report as forged. In fact, it did not have any customer with Vikrant's phone number as the registered one.

With the authenticity of each document produced by Shalini failing, my trust on her took a blow. She had failed all the three tests I subjected her to. There was one more astounding discovery when I then ran a check on Mahesh. He was Shalini's senior from college. However, she had never mentioned it to me.

Whatever I had found was a punch to my throat. The facts were beyond my understanding and seemed like puzzle pieces scattered around. It was time to take inner Abby's help to put the pieces together and comprehend what exactly was going on.

"I can think of two reasons why Shalini would fudge the documents to prove Myra was carrying Vikrant's child. One, she was seeing a future with me. She knew I loved Myra deeply and would never exclusively be hers till I chucked Myra out of my heart forever. When Mahesh hinted at Myra's infidelity and I told her about it, she sensed the hatred for Myra in my eyes and my tone. She saw an opportunity and used that premise to forge the documents and prove his claim right so that I would move on from Myra to her with no strings attached to Myra. She made Vikrant the scapegoat.

"Two, she wanted me to withdraw the case and abandon Plan B. She knew that if I started hating Myra, I would stop pursuing

Mahesh, making way for her peaceful and safe future with me without any baggage of my past.

"But why did she choose Vikrant as the scapegoat? She knew I could have confronted him on it and she would be caught red-handed. She would have lost me forever and with it, her dream of a life with me. Why did she take that risk?" I asked inner Abby.

"She chose Vikrant because she was aware he was Myra's ex and Myra's affair with him would seem credible even for a dimwit. When she decided to manipulate the proofs, she was confident she could convince you to not take up the matter with Vikrant. And she was right, you actually didn't until you went after Mona for your revenge, which she would have never imagined. In fact, you did not even check the documents properly because of your unwavering trust on her. She knows you inside-out, Abby," inner Abby said.

"Come to think of it, her underlying intention was not wrong. I understand she did it for selfish reasons, but there is nothing wrong in a wife-to-be ensuring her husband's undivided love," I justified Shalini's actions.

"Agreed, but tell me one thing. Why did she hide the fact that Mahesh was her senior in college?" inner Abby countered.

"Being his junior in college does not necessarily imply she would know him."

"It also does not imply that she wouldn't know him. He was just a year senior to her."

"So what? I didn't know all the guys who were a year senior to me at my college. Why are you against her?"

"I am not against her as such, but I have a feeling there is something not right."

"You think too much."

"First, she wanted you to withdraw the case, abort Plan B and start afresh with her. When you acquiesced and everything seemed fine, she suddenly took a U-turn and started convincing you to murder Mahesh. There's definitely something fishy."

"Let's give her the benefit of doubt. What if Mahesh was threatening her and she just complied? Maybe, she forged the documents at his behest. When we used to meet, I had noticed multiple times that she was stressed because of some reason, though she didn't tell me when I asked her, remember?"

"Yeah, I do remember. But..."

"Oh come on! She had clearly mentioned that she would have safety concerns about our kids and me throughout our lives if we didn't get rid of Mahesh. His threats must have left indelible scars on her mind and might still be haunting her. That is why she must have taken a U-turn. Isn't that a valid point?"

"It is, kind of. But I fail to understand why she wouldn't tell you about the threats."

"Because Mahesh would have threatened her with catastrophic consequences if she told anyone including me about it. You know there are so many cases where victims don't tell the police or anyone else about a crime like a ransom call for kidnapping, an extortion threat or a rape, just because they are scared of the repercussions they are intimidated with."

"That argument would have worked if Plan B wasn't on for her. Since she has already decided to go for the kill, I can't think of any reason why she wouldn't tell you about the threats now."

"If she told me about them, she would also have to admit to playing a part in maligning Myra's character and withholding information. She might be apprehensive of losing me if that came to light."

"You are an epitome of an extreme case of unconditional support."

"Call me whatever! Do you agree that she loves me?"

"Yes, I do."

"Then let's stop thinking so much."

"When you were kidnapped, Mahesh had said that Myra was up to something while you were busy slogging and selling your dream (Eduwiser) off to buy her a dream penthouse in Dubai," inner Abby disregarded my advice.

"Yes, he had."

"How did he know about that? Besides Myra and you, there was only one person who knew about it."

"Shalini?"

"Yes! Myra is no more and I don't think she had interacted with Mahesh when she was alive. You didn't tell Mahesh about it. It is only Shalini who would have done that. They were in touch, Abby."

"Obviously, they were in touch because he had been threatening her."

"Or, Shalini was hand-in-glove with him and they recently had a fallout because of which she now wants him dead," inner Abby made a valid point.

"You are corrupting my brain."

"Don't be blind in love, think neutrally. That is as valid a scenario as the one you are projecting, if not more."

"Point taken, but why would Shalini be in cahoots with Mahesh?"

"I don't know. Maybe, she wanted to save him from you. I have a feeling she is hiding more than what we can imagine, and

it is imperative that she comes out clean. I also can't help but think of a fleeting possibility."

"What possibility?"

"There is a fleeting possibility that Mahesh's allegations about Myra and Shalini producing corroborating evidence was just their game plan to malign Myra and coax you into withdrawing the case. Myra might be innocent Abby and she deserves a chance to be proved so. You should do everything in your capacity to confirm it, because if you don't, and Myra was actually virtuous, it would be very unfair for such a pure soul to bear the hatred you have in your heart. Her soul will never be able to rest in peace."

"How did I miss that point? I will do anything to prove Myra's innocence, even if there is the slightest chance of it," the words slipped out of my mouth with my eyes turning moist at that iota of hope.

"This is all very confusing. Two scenarios, exactly opposite to each other and I don't know which one is true. What do we do?" I tried to get back my composure.

"This entire puzzle has one missing piece and that piece is with Shalini. We will have to confront her."

"Should I go to Pune right away?"

"No, do not work in haste. Let's think only about what our next step should be. I am sure our next step will light up the pathway ahead for our subsequent steps and give us a chance to accost her at the right time."

"What should be our next step?"

"See, if your scenario is true, Shalini's mental peace should be your responsibility, which means you will need to get rid of Mahesh. If my scenario is true and Myra is innocent, you need

to relieve the world of Mahesh as a retribution for his misdeeds while meting out a suitable punishment for Shalini. So, in both the scenarios, Mahesh has to die."

"That seems logical."

"Play along with Shalini's wish of killing Mahesh. At least you won't have to commit the felony alone and you will have a good help in her, at your disposal."

"Makes sense," I signed off with much more clarity in what I should do next.

Conversation with the inner Abby steered my mind out of its paralysis and as soon as that happened, I called Shalini.

"Congratulations sweetheart!" I said as soon as she answered the call.

"Sweetheart? Someone's in the mood today. What happened? Why are you congratulating me?"

"You have managed to coax me into going ahead with Plan B. I thought really long and hard. Your points make sense and there were some add-on reasons as well. Thank you for reminding me the promise I had made to Rey about punishing this villain of our lives. It's not about Myra; it's about Rey and my would-be wife's mental peace. I am with you on it. Let's be partners in this crime and ship this devil to hell with a non-negotiable no-return policy. But we will need a tight plan so that we escape unharmed."

"Finally! I knew you would see sense in it. Your decision will pass as a decent Valentine's Day gift for me. I love you! Let's be on it at once," Shalini was clearly happy.

"Yeah, to kick off things, let's watch as many crime shows and unresolved murder cases as possible on YouTube and various OTT platforms, and carry out extensive research on the internet to look for ways to murder without being caught. Make sure you are logged out while doing so."

"On it, sir!" she said, ending the call.

CHAPTER 16

Location: Mumbai
Time: February 2020 - March 2020

The next one week was spent in binge-watching movies, web series, YouTube videos, etc., and browsing various news articles on murders to find our modus operandi that would fit our case and enable us to pull off the biggest coup of our lives, leaving no trace of evidence.

Planning and executing a murder seamlessly is never easy when you actually have to do it and being a first-timer makes things worse. While we came across innovative ways to murder (like using apple seeds that contain cyanide as poison, etc.), a critical analysis of such ways revealed that their execution was loaded with risks and loopholes that would work in reel life, not in real. Quite a few unsolved or incorrectly solved, real-life murder cases had the undue pressure of politicians, gangs (local or underworld) or obscenely rich people who would either threaten/bribe the investigating and forensic officers to tamper the evidence in their favour or threaten the family members of the victim to not pursue the case, just like Mahesh did to me in Myra's case. For common people like Shalini and me, it was practically impossible to escape if we managed to kill a big-shot like Mahesh, unless we had the backing of a more powerful politician, which we didn't. For that matter, even if Mahesh was murdered by any of his other enemies, I would be the prime suspect since I had a relevant motive; I had pressed charges against him for my wife's murder and was apparently forced to withdraw the case to let him walk free.

However, what needed to be done had to be done and there was no backing off. In majority of the cases I researched, murdering first and then wiping off the proofs was the norm. So, I started thinking on those lines and was immediately confronted with a number of key questions that needed answers. First, how would we assassinate him? Would we stab him with a knife, shoot him to death, poison him, throw him off a cliff, run a car over him or just fuck him to death? With no experience under our belt, all methods were difficult in their own big ways and the mere thought of executing any of them gave me cold sweat and nausea with shudders down my body.

Another pertinent question was – where would we terminate him? The crime scene could lead the police or the investigation agencies to sniff their way to us with the tiniest of evidences. So, we had to carefully decide the coordinates of the crime scene where he would be alone and unsuspecting, a place that could be cleaned patiently and thoroughly after the crime. Given that he was an affluent guy, he would always have servants, stooges and bodyguards around. Such people are never alone. Even if we did succeed in finding an ideal spot for our coronation as cold-blooded murderers, how would we accost him?

Scrutinizing some unsolved murder plots had apparently finalized the key ingredient of our barbaric plan. If Mahesh's body was found after his murder, the autopsy might reveal things that we would not be able to manipulate. So, the body had to vanish. How? Well, that was the next big question we had to find an answer to. Making a dead body vanish is not a piece of cake when you are the one who has to do it. Chopping the body into parts and disposing, burying or burning it might seem like the easiest way out, but let me enlighten you that the recent developments in the field of forensics make that extremely difficult. There have been murder cases that have been solved even after a decade, owing to the DNA technology. Also, transporting a chopped body to the disposal site without being noticed by people or CCTV cameras looks good only in movies. In reality, it is almost impossible and inevitably leaves a string of evidences. And when you are expected to be the prime suspect, it becomes an open and shut case.

There were other questions as well. Should we involve seasoned criminals or hire a hitman to do the job for us? Should we get some trustworthy friends to help or suggest? Should we explore the dark web? There were a number of options, each with its own set of parameters and loose ends without definite solutions, and that threw my mind in a hall of mirrors. Only inner Abby was competent enough to resolve the turmoil in my head that was driving me nuts.

"*Stop researching on the internet for that perfect murder case. It will only confuse you,*" inner Abby instructed.

"*But then, how will we exterminate him?*" I asked.

"*If you ever find that perfect murder case you are searching for, it would have been planned by a human mind. If anyone else could plan such a crime, why can't you? What makes you think you can't plan one from scratch? You have sufficient knowledge and intelligence to do that."*

"Thanks for the motivation, but where do I start?"

"You have an information overload, nothing else. Never overlook the power of simplicity. Keep things basic and simple."

"Can you stop beating around the bush and tell me exactly what I should do next?"

"With an open mind, learn about your enemy. Start with his social media accounts. That will give you a peek into his life. Tail him for a week or two and you will find more about him."

"And what do I do with that information?"

"Every person on earth has some or the other weakness and you need to tap into that to use it to your advantage. Don't get into the planning right now. We will cross that bridge when we get there. For now, do what I have asked you to and keep taking mental notes."

For the next two weeks, I picked up a new rental car each day and constantly followed Mahesh's car while keeping a safe distance from it to avoid suspicion. His lifestyle was similar to most of the rich and spoiled brats of Mumbai. He frequented an upscale gym and a couple of coffee shops during the day, and elite night clubs during the night. Most of the times, he was accompanied by his driver and a bodyguard and there was no pattern as to when he went out alone.

However, my driving job did not go waste because there was an interesting observation. After his weekend parties at night clubs, he went to a lodge type of place in Colaba (South Mumbai) for about ten minutes before leaving for home. Since I was curious to know about the lodge, I ventured straight into it one night, after the stipulated two weeks of my driving duty were over.

The lodge was a dingy place with no lift. The stairs weren't properly lit and were surrounded by dark, gloomy walls. On my way upstairs, I noticed a white couple smoking in the staircase area and wondered what foreigners were doing in such a shabby hostel. A familiar skunk odour confirmed they were smoking spliff. My mind automatically started building a hypothesis. Another bearded man who seemed to have passed out sitting on the stairs leaning sideways on the wall, bolstered my conjecture.

I kept climbing the stairs without a perceivable pause. There was a long gallery on the first floor, with rooms on its left side and a wall with grilled windows (facing the road) on the right. I entered the first room, the door to which was open. The room was unusually large for a city like Mumbai. In the smoke-filled ambience of the room with dim-yellow lighting, I could see a bunch of disheveled men who seemed lost in their own world. I tried asking them about the place, but couldn't comprehend what they babbled in reply, beyond one word – *maal.* Maal is a pseudonym for *stuff,* meaning drugs or narcotics and this, in conjunction with the stench and everyone's behaviour there, confirmed my hypothesis. The lodge was a den of drugs and my nemesis was probably its regular consumer; maybe, even addicted to it. The moment I got my confirmation, I scurried my way out of the place to avoid any uninvited trouble. Why did a place like this exist without being raided and cleansed by the concerned officials? Your guess would be as good as mine – money and powerful people! Everyone from top to bottom got a cut to help such places thrive almost openly. Whatever the case, it was not my concern. What mattered the most to me was that I had zeroed in on a critical weakness of Mahesh – dope – and it was time to discuss the way forward with the inner Abby.

"*I found one weakness of Mahesh. How do we use that against him?*" I asked.

"*The one you found is the second weakness. The first one is the universal weakness of all men, and that is women. Both these weaknesses have almost frozen the crucial components of our plan. Don't get distracted by other parameters now,*" inner Abby outlined.

"*Alright! Now to use his first weakness against him, we will need to set up a honey-trap and for that, we will need a woman,*" I deduced.

"*Correct.*"

"*But I can't risk involving anyone else in this plan, apart from Shalini and me.*"

"*Who is asking you to?*"

"*You mean, Shalini?*"

"*Yes, 'use and throw'. I think she will turn out to be a disposable resource who you will have to get rid of, if you want to live happily ever after in peace. I say this because I firmly believe she was playing from Mahesh's side in some capacity and trying to sabotage your revenge. I suggest, murder Mahesh and frame Shalini for it. Don't forget to assassinate her character. You don't have to be the 'kind' guy all the time. Sometimes, you have to be selfish and cruel. That's life.*"

"*Why do you keep crapping against her and suggest things that make me look like the worst villain ever?*"

"It depends on the point of reference from where one looks at things. A hero is a villain from the villain's point of view, right?"

"Right, but we will see. We don't have a definite confirmation yet, on her involvement with Mahesh. I will give her a chance to come out clean regardless of your pressure to dispose her off. If at all she was involved with him in any capacity, her punishment will be commensurate with her extent of involvement. Anyway, I am fine with Shalini being the 'honey' in our honey trap. That brings us to my next question. How do we use his second weakness? Do we even need to?"

"Of course, you will need to. How else would the 'honey' in the plan debilitate a hefty guy like Mahesh for you guys to proceed with the murder?"

"Ok, what drug do we use and how do we source it?"

"Keep it simple. Search on Google for the party drug that is most frequently used and source it from the Colaba lodge you visited. Remember to do all online searches in incognito mode to prevent being tracked."

"Understood. Where will we kill him? Should we choose a local hotel, an outstation one or some Airbnb property that Shalini can convince Mahesh to book, after trapping him?"

"You need to reduce the number of unknowns or variables, not increase them. Don't add an unknown hotel or Airbnb property and hence, a truckload of people (as witnesses), to the plan. These people and the CCTV surveillance at these places will only get you trapped. Execute the killing at Mahesh's apartment."

"At his apartment? You must be kidding me."

"I am serious."

"How on earth will we be able to break into his apartment?"

"Talk to Shalini. From what we know, she has been in direct touch with Mahesh (in both our scenarios), and it should be a cakewalk for her."

"Hmm... After making Mahesh powerless with a strong dose of the drug, how do we kill him eventually?"

"That will be your choice. Keep in mind that at least in India, the cops form an initial assumption of the crime based on their first impression at the crime scene. After that, their entire team works to find proofs to fortify their initial assumption. They do not look at other possibilities, though they claim to. If you are able to contaminate the crime scene in such a way that it forces the investigators to form an initial assumption of a story you would want them to believe, rest assured they will end up proving what you want them to prove, without you stressing over it. You are an author. You better think of a good story because a bad one, or even a decent one for that matter, will put you behind bars for a long, long time."

"Even if I manage to think of a credible story, outwitting the forensics team armed with the latest DNA technology seems impossible."

"Use the DNA technology to your advantage, leading the cops and the forensics into believing the story you want them to."

"Ok. What about disposing the dead body?"

"You don't have to get rid of the body. The moment you start moving around with the dead body to dispose it off, you will leave traces of evidence that will ultimately lead the cops to you, sooner or even years later. We should close this chapter once and for all, right after Mahesh's death. For that, the body should be discovered and his death should be confirmed. Needless to

mention, the state of the dead body and the crime scene should be consistent with one another and your story."

"So, the success of this plan depends solely on the story I create? My head is spinning!"

"Grab some sleep and then, start thinking of the plot. You are gifted with that ability."

The conversation with the inner Abby was like a flashlight piercing through the dense fog of information overload and confusion in my mind, revealing the logically obvious next step in my strategy.

I loved Shalini deeply, but whether or not she would have to be a perishable character in my story for the investigators and the outside world, only destiny knew.

CHAPTER 17

Location: Mumbai
Time: March 2020 - June 2020

I had to think of not one, but two plans. Both had to protect me indubitably. However, the first had to ensure that Shalini would be safe and not suspected for the murder even vaguely because I had to spend the rest of my life with her, while the second had to ensure the exact opposite. Whether or not the second plan would come into effect would have to be decided on the spur of the moment after we took care of Mahesh. Obviously, there had to be two stories to be thought of, one for each plan, and evidences had to be accordingly tampered to mislead the investigation. And that further complicated things for me.

Putting my thinking skills to an ultimate weeklong test, I came up with both the plans. Though half-baked, the first and the only plan I apprised Shalini of, convinced her, and she instantly came onboard. As expected, she sounded confident of pulling the *honey's* character off. For the remainder part of the plan, she had apprehensions, but her complete trust on my execution was enough to somewhat take care of them.

The plan was simple – I would drop Shalini at a spot in Mumbai from where Mahesh would pick her up and take her home. She would then spike his drinks with a drug while I would wait on the street right outside his society. Once he passed out, she would signal to me and I would enter the scene to administer the overdose (if needed) to kill him, once and for all. Shalini and I would then escape after cleaning his apartment and getting rid of all proofs – physical and digital (from Mahesh's phone and other electronic devices). The story for the world would be that Mahesh died due to a drug overdose.

"How does the plan sound?" I asked her.

"It sounds good. But I am nervous," she said.

"Which part is making you nervous?"

"I will be entering the building with Mahesh. The security as well as the CCTV footage would confirm my presence with him. We will easily get trapped. The same concern will be there when we leave together after killing Mahesh."

"I have already thought about these concerns and done the required recce to address them. In Mahesh's building, there is just one apartment on every floor. The parking for every resident is on the same floor as his apartment. A resident's car can go up the elevator to his parking. So, when you enter Mahesh's society and then his building, you will not have to get down from the car. With slight effort, you can easily escape the CCTV cameras and the eyes of the security personnel in the society.

Most buildings here, including Mahesh's, have a rear gate for loading/unloading of oversized stuff like sofas, refrigerators, etc. This gate is unmanned and at least in Mahesh's building, there is no CCTV camera installed there. I didn't check in other buildings as there was no point. I will be entering the building through this gate and after we finish our job, we will use the same gate to exit. Does that take care of your concerns?" I explained to her.

"To a great extent but I am still skittish about the second part. What if something goes wrong? If the main gate security does not allow you to enter Mahesh's society for some reason, how will I handle things alone? What if someone arrives during the operation? We might end up getting killed," she expressed her reservations.

"The problem is we don't have enough options. We will have to take some risks."

"Hmm...," she was still unsure.

"Do you trust me?"

"You know I do."

"Nothing will go wrong and if at all anything does, I will take care of it. Nothing in this world will be able to stop me from entering Mahesh's house when you signal me to. I will not leave you alone, baby. I will be right outside his society. And once I am there inside the house, I will take charge while you can sit and relax.

If you have to worry about something, it should be the first part. How will you befriend Mahesh? Will you use a pseudonym or your real identity? You will have to reveal your original identity because he might not take you home if you don't. But if you reveal your identity, why would he be interested in you?"

"That's my work and I will handle it. Don't stress about it. You focus on the second part of the plan," she assured me.

"I will be more than happy to. How much time will it take you to wheedle him?"

"How much time do you want me to take?"

"One week?"

"Done!"

"What? I said one week sarcastically because I am not the best person to decide on the timeframe for that particular objective, you are. How will you lure him and gain his trust in just one week? There is no scope of failure here. So, don't be in a rush to get the monkey off your back."

"Trust me, like I trust you."

"Yeah, why not! Let's get things cranking then."

Each of us spent the next few days fine-tuning and mentally preparing for our respective own part. We switched to WhatsApp for our calls to be on the safer side. We exchanged messages on WhatsApp about general stuff, but never wrote a word about Mahesh or our plan. As a side hustle, I was also fine-tuning my second plan that she wasn't privy to.

26 March was the date finalized for the strike. It was a Thursday, a weekday when we wouldn't encounter *nakabandi* by cops late at night (on our way back after executing Mahesh), which is always there on Friday and Saturday nights. The society also wouldn't have people moving in and out late at night, which would mitigate our risk of having eye-witnesses. It was now time to put our money where our mouths were.

All this while, we were so caught up in our planning that a global crisis had completely skipped our attention or maybe, we considered it too inconsequential to pay any heed to. It was the Covid-19 pandemic that started as a tiny wave in China in November 2019, but had now grown humongous enough to engulf the entire world. The contagiousness of the disease was unprecedented and its effects were so deadly that the Prime Minister of India was forced to announce a twenty-one-day nationwide lockdown on 24 March. The lockdown wasn't unique to India; other countries were in the same boat. Every person, including me, was scared for loved ones' lives. The fact that there was no prior knowledge about the causative Corona virus (that would keep mutating) and no medicine to cure the disease, the pandemic was already en route to become one of the worst ever in the history of mankind. As a result, we were forced to postpone our plan till things got better.

Since Rey wasn't with me, I was initially worried about him. But thanks to my parents and the video-calling technology, I was soon at peace. Living with his VIP grandparents in a huge bungalow with garden all around it, and with ample staff to run errands for them, the lockdown wasn't expected to affect him as much as it would affect millions of others who were confined within the four walls of their humble abodes.

Shalini was in Pune with Sia and her parents. I was in regular touch with her to help her keep calm and to assure her that I was there to support whenever she needed it, despite being in two minds about her.

A couple of weeks into the lockdown, our tornado of panic abated. Travelling was still not possible, not only because it was not allowed, but also because we needed to shield ourselves from the highly contagious infection. Infection was almost a certainty if anyone dared to venture out of his home. With food supplies and other grocery items stocked up, we were self-sufficient in our respective homes and we just had to vile away some time before we could find another suitable time to execute our plan.

There were innumerable negatives of the pandemic playing spoilsport and hitting the world at the wrong time, at least for us. We would have been through with our plan had the lockdown happened a couple of weeks later. There couldn't have been a worse party-pooper. But being an incorrigible optimist, I could not help but notice multiple silver streaks to the dark cloud. One, I got more time to think about my second plan to make it infallible and impervious to failure. Two, the pandemic was there to stay and it meant even less or no eye-witnesses. Three, the cops and the security guys were scared for their lives themselves and they kept indoors. And if they were forced to go out by their superiors to control the spread of the pandemic, they kept their distance from people. Four, the use of masks was made mandatory and wearing PPE (Personal Protective Equipment) kits to cover the entire body was considered normal, both of which made it almost impossible for people to recognize and pin-point anyone. Last but not the least, Shalini got more time to build trust with Mahesh, though I was not sure if that was really needed.

Despite the deafening Covid-19 noise, Shalini was diligent and committed enough to continue chatting with Mahesh to build trust. In fact, she said they had started talking to each other on phone as well. She had shared a few screenshots of her chats with him and by the looks of it, he seemed to be quite into her. The lockdown had forced abstinence from sex for bachelors like Mahesh, and it was an unbearable torture for them. I knew that by the time the lockdown would end, he would have also transformed into a sex-starved, supercharged, raging bull ready to fuck whatever hole he saw. And that would work in our favour, but only if we struck as soon as the lockdown ended. However, things were very uncertain.

After wading through multiple lockdown extensions as Covid-19 continued to tighten its grip on the mortal world and smother it into a graveyard, we got our shot more than two months later when the Government initiated Unlock 1.0 in June to lift the lockdown in a phased manner and put things back on track.

11 June was finalized as the new date for our *D-Day*. We had waited patiently with bated breaths for the last few months and were now eager to finish off the *work*. At the same time, we were a bundle of nerves knowing that a failure might transform our D-Day into the *L-Day* (last day) of our lives.

CHAPTER 18

Location: Mumbai
Time: June 2020

Despite the Unlock 1.0 already into play, the cab services were down and so was the public transport. So, on the eventful day of 11 June, I decided to drive to Pune in the afternoon to get Shalini to Mumbai. I also needed some lone time with her to drill the plan into her head and soothe her nerves so that she neither deviated from our plan nor panicked during the course of it, and the drive back to Mumbai gave me that window.

I reached Pune at about 4 p.m. To my surprise, no one stopped my car to ask why I was out during the pandemic. In fact, I didn't even have to stop at the toll gates because they were not manned. The VIP registration number and the brand of my car, alongside the fear of the deadly infection might have had their roles to play in it. Whatever the reason, I was not complaining.

I picked up Shalini from a place she had walked down to, a place where she was sure there were no CCTV cameras installed. Both of us were wearing our PPE suits to avoid the contagion as well as identification. My car's registration number would have given away my identity anyway, but if things went exactly as per my plan, it would not come to the point where the police would dig up my location or my car's, as long as I did not take my car too close to Mahesh's building. Even if I did, the police would not be able to conclusively claim that I was involved in the murder in any capacity. But like I said, all of this was conditional to my success in misleading the cops with the story I would tell through the evidences at the crime scene.

Shalini's part was limited to the first half of the plan, which was very crucial. Unfortunately, the success of that part was beyond my control and was solely dependent on her. One small mistake and there would be no turning back for us on our road to expedited death or incarceration. So, I had asked her to focus only on her part and let me take care of the latter part because I didn't want to muddle her mind up with an overload of information on intricate details of my part. She knew the crux of the entire plan, and that was about it.

"Hey, ready for action?" I held her gloved hand as she sat in the car.

"Yeah, keeping my fingers crossed," she exhaled.

"What's that uniform kind of stuff you are wearing underneath?" she asked.

"It isn't a proper uniform but it's the same colour as the BMC uniform, and this is my ID," I flashed the fake ID I had prepared. I had never thought my publishing background and hands-on knowledge of design applications would come in handy in such a situation to design a fake ID.

"I am going to enter as the BMC guy, who has to check the building for Covid cases. So, the building security won't be able to stop me, and I know they are not competent enough to authenticate the forged ID card. Though evening time is an unusual time for the BMC to check the premises, it is an emergency situation due to Covid; it should be safe, no one would raise a red flag. I have a spare set of clothes in my bag for you to change into after we get rid of Mahesh, so that you can escape easily with me, without getting identified and raising any suspicion," I added.

"Just shows I don't have to worry about your part of the plan."

"I hope you didn't tell your parents you were coming with me."

"No, I just told them I needed a break for a day to clear my head and would be back tomorrow," Shalini said.

"Good, it's advisable to not have met today in the eyes of any third person. Time to switch off our phones to avoid leaving any electronic trail of today's whereabouts. Just in case the police sense foul play in Mahesh's death and investigate, I don't want our devices to pin-point our location to Mahesh's apartment or even in Mumbai today, for that matter."

"Yeah."

"Wait a minute. Before you switch off your phone, call Mahesh over WhatsApp to reconfirm the time and location of your pick-up. Tell him that you are on your way to Mumbai and might not be able to call him when you reach the pick-up location because your phone is discharged and will die any moment."

"Sure."

"I believe you have already asked him to send his servant out for the night. Check with him on that and tell him you are not going to stay the night if his servant or anyone else is going to be there at his home, because that will invade your privacy. I am sure he is so much into you that he is going to vacate not just living things but also the furniture out of his house to spend the night with you."

Shalini called Mahesh and did the needful before switching off the phone. The pick-up location was a spot in Juhu previously recced by me to ensure there were no CCTV cameras installed there.

"Have you got the drug?" she asked.

"Yes, here it is, 2 mg each," I handed over five sachets, each filled with 2 mg of powder.

"What drug is this?" she asked as she stowed away the sachets in a hidden pocket of her purse.

"This is Rohypnol, popularly known as roofies, forget-me drug or date-rape drug. It is a CNS (Central Nervous System) depressant that slows down heart rate, suppresses respiration and impairs an individual within twenty minutes of administration for about four to six hours with just 1 mg dosage," I enlightened her.

"Why have you made sachets of 2 mg?"

"The dosage and the corresponding intensity of effects of this drug depend on the built of an individual. For a guy like Mahesh, 10 mg will definitely be a fatal overdose; 2 mg will not kill him but would guarantee his collapse, and 1 mg might not suffice," I explained to her.

"Why not give him an overdose in one shot and kill him?"

"Good point, but there is a catch in that. If we put more than 2 mg in one drink, the drink might taste a little salty and Mahesh could get suspicious. We can't afford that goof-up. Though I am giving you five sachets of 2 mg each, you will most likely be able to use just one because he would pass out with the first drink itself, before you serve him his second one."

"How will I administer the remaining four doses after he has passed out?"

"I will take care of that. As discussed before, once he passes out, switch the living room light on and off thrice. That will be my cue to enter the scene and do the honours with the remaining doses to freeze all his vital functions and stall his breathing forever. Remember, do not call or message me."

"Ok. Where will you be while I am busy with my part of the plan?"

"Like I had said, I will be on the road right outside his society and have my eyes fixed on his living room window, waiting for your signal. I know the place on the road from where I will have a direct view of his apartment."

"What I have to do will not take ten or fifteen minutes. It will take time. Standing on the street and staring at Mahesh's living room window continuously for a long time is sure to raise some eyebrows, apart from being impractical for you," Shalini raised her concern.

"You are right. Let's estimate the duration of the first part of operation. It will take about twenty minutes for you guys to reach his apartment from Juhu. Once you guys reach his apartment, an hour should be enough to wrap up initial guesting formalities, prepare the first spiked drink and finish it off. Add thirty minutes of waiting time for him to pass out. So, a total of about two hours. From the time he picks you up, I will start waiting for your signal after two hours. Does that sound good?"

"Make that two and a half hours instead of two, because I will need additional time to find that opportune moment when I can spike his drink."

"Two and a half hours it is. Shalini, I am a little worried."

"About what?"

"What if Mahesh doesn't take the spiked drink for some reason?"

"Don't worry, I will manage," Shalini was confident.

"Though it is not that important, but since we still have an hour to our destination, I wanted to ask you something I didn't understand."

"What?"

"How did you manage to trap Mahesh despite him knowing that you are close to me? Why did he fall for you?"

"Almost every man will fall for a woman. All she needs to do is give him what he wants, virtually or in-person."

"You met him?"

"Of course not, but I did engage in wild chats with him to lure him into me."

"But he doesn't have dearth of beautiful women to have wild chats with or fuck around with. Why would he choose his enemy?"

"I am sure you too don't have paucity of hotter women to make love to, but you chose me, right? So, there must be something special in me."

"My case is different. I have loved you for close to two decades."

"How does it matter, Abby? It is not important. Maybe, he is a weirdo who fantasizes fucking his enemies literally, and gets a 'high' out of it. Or maybe, he wants to get back at you by sleeping with your woman, which is me!"

I gave Shalini a chance to tell me she knew Mahesh from before, but she didn't. I was finding it hard to justify her still being tight-lipped about it, given that we were about to execute him. She could have at least told me about having interacted with him before. What was also clear was that she wouldn't reveal anything in a straight forward way and I would have to use force to make her spill the secrets she was so religiously guarding.

Somewhere in my heart, the scale had now almost completely tilted in favour of inner Abby's proposed scenario. And in that case, my default plan was to frame her for Mahesh's murder. There were chances she would try to disclose my involvement in it, but the law would only believe in the evidences which I would ensure would be all stacked against her, not me. She would be like most of the accused who keep pleading that they are innocent, but nobody pays heed to their claims.

I didn't question her further about Mahesh, because if she had been on the same team as him, at least during the trial, she would get suspicious. My mission would then go down the drain and I would never get my hands on the truth. Moreover, she could team up with Mahesh after meeting him and kill me instead. Nonetheless, as long as there was non-zero probability of her being innocent, I wouldn't deny her the chance to tell her side of the story and come out clean.

CHAPTER 19

Location: Mumbai
Time: June 2020

I dropped Shalini a few hundred metres away from her pick-up location at around 7 p.m. and parked my car in one of the bylanes to walk to a place from where I could have an unobstructed view of the pick-up point. Half an hour later, a white Range Rover pulled over in front of Shalini and she got in. I could recognize the bastard on the driver's seat even with his mask on.

"Your last few hours in this world, Mahesh. The universe will thank me for what I will do to you tonight!" I whispered in the air.

I drove to my society to park my car somewhere near it, after which I took an auto-rickshaw and dropped off about a kilometre away from Mahesh's society that was about three kilometres from mine. I walked to my final spot on the street with my companion – a bag. The bag had a butcher knife, white vinegar, cotton buds, soda water, a couple of Red Bull cans, about 50 mg of Rohypnol, spare BMC uniform, nylon ropes, two pairs of kinky handcuffs and blindfold ordered from a leading lingerie brand and other stuff that would come in handy while setting up the crime scene in my favour.

I still had about two hours to go before Shalini would signal for me to enter. Sitting on a low running wall along the pavement, I couldn't help but wonder how my life had come to this. Barely registering the activity around me, I sifted through memories of Myra, Shalini and Rey. Life was so good when I was with Myra and Rey. With an incredible background, a promising career and an ideal wife (apparently) with a loving son, I was a thing of envy for most in the world. And here I was, waiting on the roadside to commit a murder. None could have imagined I would be standing at such a crossroad.

There were a number of questions boiling in my heart and bubbling up to my mind. Was the current situation avoidable? What I was going to commit in the next few hours, was it really worth it? Myra was no more and whatever I did, she would never come back. Rey's life would be completely ruined if there was even the slightest of misses from me. Was there any point in digging up the past and reconciling things? Shalini had awakened a renewed commitment in me to rebuild my family with her and I was happy about it. Did I need to get into all this and complicate our lives, making them tougher? These questions could be partly attributed to the fact that in theory, everything I was going to do seemed easy-peasy; but in practice, it was literally scaring the shit out of me and giving me cold feet.

The spate of thoughts was conspiring to fog my mind and chase it out of the plan. I was feeling terribly sick but what had to be done, had to be done. Mahesh had to be dispatched to hell and there were no two ways about it. And if Shalini was associated with Mahesh and was protecting him for whatever reasons, she was guilty of obstruction of justice as well as slandering Myra with mala fide intentions, and had to be suitably punished too, as per my default plan.

But I wanted Shalini to be innocent because I genuinely wished to share my life with her. As I waited eagerly for her signal, I started praying fervently to the universe for the best-case scenario in which Mahesh would be murdered smoothly and both, Myra and Shalini would emerge guiltless. I didn't have to wait too long. The lights turned on and off thrice at 9.30 p.m., half an hour before the stipulated time. I believe the universe too was getting impatient for the secret pages of my life to unfold.

On my way to Mahesh's apartment, I encountered CCTV cameras at the society entrance, but I was cool with it. No one could recognize me from underneath the BMC uniform, the PPE suit and a face mask. The entry gate was manned by a security personnel, but he didn't ask me the apartment number I was headed to when I flashed my ID and told him I was from the BMC. As per the plan, I entered Mahesh's building through the rear gate and took the stairs to his apartment to avoid CCTV cameras in the lifts.

Clung onto the hope of the best-case scenario, I knocked at Mahesh's door with my gloved hand. I would be lying if I said I trusted Shalini completely at that point to not double-cross me. Somewhere in my mind, I was kind of expecting an unpleasant surprise of meeting a sober and furious Mahesh, who would have my balls nailed to his living room wall for daring to plan his assassination.

When Shalini opened the door (after confirming through the view-finder that it was me), I glanced at her panic-stricken face and then peered inside through the partially opened door to check if Mahesh was down and out. The sight of a passed-out Mahesh on the living room couch relieved the pressure off my lungs and I sighed.

"All good?" I returned my gaze to a nervous, crumple-faced Shalini.

"Come in," she mouthed without a decibel of sound.

"What's wrong? He passed out, right?" I whispered to reconfirm.

"Yeah!"

"Well done! I think that was the most difficult part of the plan and you nailed it," I complimented.

"Did you check for the security cameras in the house?" I asked without waiting for her response.

"I asked Mahesh to turn them off before I entered his house and he complied. I confirmed it as soon as I stepped inside," she assured with a quaking voice.

"That was smooth."

"I am nervous, Abby. I obviously had to remove my PPE suit and gloves when I came here. I have touched multiple things, including Mahesh, and my fingerprints are all over the place. We will get caught," she mumbled in fear and trepidation.

"Relax Shalini, get a grip on yourself. I am here now and I will take care of everything. You come and sit here," I made her sit on the couch.

"Take deep breaths," I instructed her and checked on Mahesh.

"I gave him his second drink because he had the first one laced with one sachet very quickly," she babbled.

"Fair enough. He is still breathing, but I guess those are his last few breaths," I checked his body.

"We will need to delete my call records and chat history from his phone," Shalini said nervously.

"Yes, we will delete all your calls and messages from his phone, except the normal calls. Normal call records should not be deleted from his phone because the cops will get to know the details from the telecom operator anyway. If we delete such calls from his call log and the cops dig it up from the backend, it might raise unwanted suspicion. I don't think you guys interacted over a normal call today. So, we are good. Call records from before can't prove that you were with him tonight. Your phone is switched off and no one can track your location electronically. Do not turn it on till you reach Pune. You were in Pune today; get that fact drilled deep into your head."

"I can't think clearly. My brain is not working," she broke into cold sweat.

"I am there na Shalini, like you have always been there for me," I kneeled before her.

"We have at least eight hours in our hands before sunrise to wipe out all the proofs and walk out through the exit gate of the society. And we will be free from Mahesh's fear forever.

"It's 9.45 p.m. We are ahead of our target time. Let's take a break and use it to calm down. Give me a minute, I will get you a can of Red Bull. It will help in boosting your mind and body," I said and got up to fetch the can from my bag.

"Thanks, Abby," she said looking into my eyes helplessly.

While I *prepared* her can, she was busy staring at the night sky through the French windows of the living room, as if praying to the stars to help us get through unscarred, at the earliest possible.

"Here, have this," I interrupted her thoughts.

"What took you so long?"

"The white vinegar I had brought to wipe off the fingerprints, had spilled a little. I was just cleaning it."

Twenty minutes later, I noticed Shalini starting to feel dizzy as I watched her from a distance. About half an mg of Rohypnol that I had laced her Red Bull with, had started to kick in. She wanted to get up and walk to me, but her ankles rolled, making her fall back on the couch. Gradually, her other muscles too declined to co-operate and give wings to her effort. A few minutes later, she was physically and mentally impaired, unable to move and disconnected with reality. All she could do was mumble incoherently and relentlessly, and I let her do that for the next one hour, which I used to survey Mahesh's apartment and ready myself for her interrogation.

Mahesh's was a four-bedroom apartment. One of the bedrooms had an office type of set-up, while the other three were proper bedrooms with beds. Luckily, one of those three bedrooms had a bed with canopy bed curtains and vertical rods at the corners. Or, I would have to use the dining chairs from the living room to serve my purpose.

After an hour of her slurry blabbering, I lifted her off the couch and carried her to this bedroom while she continued muttering. With the two pairs of handcuffs I had brought, I restrained her fully-stretched hands, one to each of the two corners on the head-side of the queen-size bed as she laid flat on it. I tied her spread out legs to the remaining two corners on the foot-side, using nylon ropes.

Her impaired judgement due to the small dosage of the drug was not letting her comprehend what was going on. As she subconsciously squirmed to free herself, I further pinned her to the bed with my knees on either side of her waist and hands on either side of her shoulders, my face so close to hers that I could smell the irresistible fragrance of her breath.

With my butcher knife at my disposal to intimidate her, should there be a need, it was now time to hear everything from the horse's mouth. My moment of truth had arrived.

CHAPTER 20

Location: Mumbai
Time: June 2020

"I have some doubts that I want you to clarify and I want straight forward answers. Why did you forge Myra's phone bills, Vikrant's hotel bills and the pregnancy test report?" I started my interrogation and cut straight to the chase.

"Mmm...Mai nana nu you," she mumbled.

"Talk properly!" I slapped right across her face to wake her up from her state of delirium, my impatience to be blamed. We were at the crime scene and I had tons of work to do after I discovered the missing piece of the puzzle. I didn't have time for her mutterings.

"Ya...ya...you (I love you)," she started whimpering.

I needed some level of sobriety in her to get my answers, but she wasn't out of her ecstasy yet. It would take some more time for the effects of the drug to abate just a little bit more so that she could talk more coherently. Thankfully, I knew the trick and was carrying the solution to this problem in my bag to expedite her return to just the right level of her senses.

I splashed her face relentlessly with the soda from the two soda bottles I had brought. Each splash made her flinch, accelerating her journey on the road to limited recovery.

"No, no, nooo!" she finally spoke something I could fathom. The splashing of soda had probably annoyed her to no end, but her volume was still low.

She tried to open her eyes, but the bright light of the room made her squint. Her red eyes frowned at me, bewildered as to where we were and why I was on top of her.

"Where are we?" she was perplexed.

"Hey, good morning! Good to have you back. We are at Mahesh's home," I answered.

"What? Why are we still here? How long has it been? What happened to me?" she fired a barrage of questions at me. She obviously didn't remember what had happened in the last couple of hours or so.

"To give you a sense of time, it is 12.30 a.m. You were panicking a lot. So, I *roofied* you to calm you down," I replied.

"Why have you tied my hands and legs? What are you up to? Untie me," her slithering to free her limbs gave way to a struggle, with a sudden realization that she was constrained. She moaned like a zombie and tried to squeal for help, but all she could let out was a low-sounding grunt.

"Stop struggling and relax, you will hurt yourself," I didn't want her to get bruised.

"Why are you doing this to me? Wait, am I still hallucinating?" she wasn't ready to believe the ongoing.

"No, you are not, but everything is fine and in control. I just need you to clarify some of my doubts," I tried to calm her down.

"What clarification? And is this the way to get it? Are you out of your fucking mind? Let go of me at once," her volume started increasing as her condition took rapid strides towards sobriety.

I grabbed her hair at the back of her head with my left hand while pointing the knife to her face with my right hand, to remind her who the *Daddy* was in the given situation.

"You increase your volume or shout for help, this knife will cut right through your face. It will be very convenient for me to put Mahesh's fingerprint on it and walk out. So, keep your decibels down," I threatened.

"Alright, alright...I will co-operate. Ask me," she surrendered instantaneously.

"Why did you forge Myra's phone bills, Vikrant's hotel bills and the pregnancy test report?" I resumed my interrogation.

"I...I didn't. Why will I do that?" she feigned innocence.

"I have verified their authenticity. They are fake."

"Ah...umm," she was searching for answers.

"Myra was not pregnant with Vikrant's child," I yelled at her.

"Ok, let me explain. I loved you and wanted to marry you. The feeling was mutual, but you were always pre-occupied with Myra. I wanted her out of your life so that I could have your undivided love and attention. There was only one way I could achieve that and that was by making sure you hated her. What Mahesh told you about her, gave me that opportunity and I doctored evidences accordingly to prove beyond doubt that she had cheated on you. I had no idea you would run a check on them," she confessed and the reason fell in line with my proposed scenario.

"You maligned Myra for your selfish reasons? Did you realize how much that hurt me?" I could feel tears beneath my eyelids.

"I agree it was selfish of me, but my intentions were not malefic. I did it only for your love."

"I did love you Shalini and I was dragging myself out of Myra's memories. You were aware of it. There was absolutely no need for what you did," I told her, completely in rage.

"I agree with you, Abby. I am so sorry."

"Why did you choose Vikrant? You could have chosen any random guy I didn't know. I knew Vikrant and could have easily confronted him. That would have blown the lid off your lies. Why did you take such a risk? I need all the details."

"I will tell you everything. You had told me Vikrant was Myra's ex, during one of our conversations. An extramarital affair with an ex always looks believable. I was confident I could convince you to not confront Vikrant on it. You, being you, would comply and you did. I knew you trusted me blindly and wouldn't think beyond what I told you. That's why it didn't take much for me to persuade you to let me do the investigation. I found Vikrant's number from Myra's contact list on her phone. Married women who have flings outside their marriages often change the contact name of their lovers to avoid suspicion from their husbands. While flitting through Myra's WhatsApp chats, I came across her childhood friend, Stuti Bangal. So, I changed Vikrant's contact name to *Stuti New* to add credibility to my story of the illegitimate affair. I also put his phone number on the phone bills as well as the forged pregnancy test report. For the hotel bills, you had told me when she had gone to Goa with her friends. I searched for the hotel bills on her email that was already configured on her phone and didn't need any password for access. I doctored that template to generate Vikrant's bills for the same hotel. The mental state that you were in, I knew the maximum you would check would be Vikrant's phone number and his name on the bills, and I had that covered," she filled me in with the details of her felony.

"You abused my trust, Shalini," I was heartbroken, though what she said was consistent with what I had expected.

"I did Abby and I understand that's the reason you have me tied up like this. It is justified. But right now, it is important for you to realize that we are on borrowed time. Let's clean up this place and leave from here. We have a lifetime with us for me to clarify things with you and make up for my mistakes. At the moment, let's just do what is priority," she tried to put me back in her groove.

It was clear Myra had not dallied with Vikrant, but had she been two-timing me with someone else? Our discussion had only scraped the surface and I was still to go deep into the facts. What unearthed as a result of it was a mind-numbing, unimaginable truth that rocked my entire being.

"We are not moving until I have all my answers," I asserted.

"I already told you everything. What else do you want to know?" Shalini was taken aback.

"Myra's case had closed and Mahesh was out of our lives. We were all set to start a new life together. Everything was good and peaceful, after a long time for me. Why did you suddenly take a U-turn on your decision, after convincing me to move on in life? Why did you suddenly want to eliminate Mahesh and pee on our lives all over again? What am I missing?"

"He was out of your life, not mine."

"What do you mean?" I was confused.

"He was threatening me."

"Threatening you? I had already withdrawn the case. There was no point in him trying to intimidate you for any reason. What did he want from you?"

"Sexual favours."

"Sexual favours? But why from you? This is funny."

"I don't know. I have already told you before, he liked fucking his enemies, maybe."

"Why didn't you tell me about it?"

"He said he would kill Sia, Rey and you if I did. I was scared," Shalini was terrified.

"Since when were you in touch with him?"

"He had contacted me after you withdrew the case."

"So, that was after my abduction."

"Right."

"You didn't know him personally before that?"

"No," she was hesitant.

"I sold my dream to realize Myra's. Only three people knew about it – Myra, me and you. How did Mahesh come to know about it?"

"How would I know?"

"Myra was not there to tell him and she didn't know him when she was alive. I didn't tell him either. It was only you, Shalini," I was stern.

"You must have blurted it out in front of him when he abducted you."

"I didn't blurt it out when he abducted me, he did, you bitch. Tell me the truth," I squeezed both her cheeks against each other, her lips forced to form a pout.

"I will tell you, wait. He began threatening me ever since we started coming close to each other, especially after our Patna trip. I believe he was keeping an eye on us. He threatened me with serious consequences if I didn't provide him with all the details about Myra and your lives, and your next move in the case. I must have mentioned to him about the penthouse too. After you withdrew the case, he started asking me for carnal favours."

"Why would he need you for the information? He was well connected and powerful enough to get all the information himself. I am not convinced. Plus, your timeline changed in a minute. Think twice and answer. One more discrepancy in what you tell me and I will let my rage unleash at you," I warned her.

"I, I, I...," she started whimpering profusely, unable to breathe and speak.

"I am giving you five minutes to calm down. When I resume my questions, you tell me nothing but the truth and you will stand a chance to walk away. But if you lie or don't answer the questions to my satisfaction, you will experience the stuff of nightmares at my hands. Is that understood?" I gave her an ultimatum, stuffing a piece of cloth in her mouth.

"Mmmm...mmm," she nodded.

I left her alone to have some lone time myself. The continuous change in her statements and timelines was confusing me. I sat on the couch and buried my face in my hands, only to inadvertently stumble upon an ace that had been up my sleeves for years, but I had no idea that would force her to lay all her cards on the table.

"It's been an hour, Shalini. We don't have much time. For the love we nurture for each other, for the lovely times we spent together, I am going to give you one more chance. Since when did you know Mahesh?" I removed the cloth from her mouth.

"Take me home Abby, for the sake of that love," she pleaded.

"Answer my fucking question!!!"

"I told you. We have been in touch since you and I started seeing each other again, after our Patna trip."

"Wasn't he your senior in college?"

"Ah! Was he? I...I didn't know that. I swear," she stammered.

"Really?"

"Yeah, I didn't even know all the guys in my batch, leave aside knowing seniors," she tried to defend.

"I called up Shweta, your best friend in college and my so-called *sister from past life*. Remember?" I told her.

"What did she tell you?" she sounded stumped.

"Everything," I bluffed. I had not called Shweta, neither was I sure that Shalini actually knew Mahesh from her college days.

"Ok," she sighed.

"Just ok?" I nudged her to enlighten me. The bluff had worked.

"I had dated Mahesh in college," she confessed while I tried to hold back my astonishment.

"Stop answering in bits and parts, and tell me the whole story," I gnashed my teeth with irritation.

"My boyfriend who disappeared on me was not Sunny, it was Mahesh."

"Oh Lord! What a night of revelation! Who was Sunny then? You had even sent me his Facebook profile link to see how he looked."

"Sunny was my batchmate who looked pretty average. Had I sent you Mahesh's pic, you would have certainly believed I dumped you for your looks."

"So you did dump me for my looks," I was shattered.

"Sorry Abby, I shouldn't have. Maybe, the long-distance thing also worked against our relationship."

"Crap! Why did you start dating me again? After your divorce, you should have gone back to him, instead."

"He had taken off on me when I had asked him to send his parents to talk to mine, for our marriage. I couldn't trust him again and I consciously avoided any touchpoint with him. By the time my divorce came through, I had also realized what a gem you were and I had fallen for you. He got back in touch after my divorce and our Patna trip, but with a different intention – of intimidating me, first with respect to the case and then for his lust. I have already told you what happened thereafter.

"In retrospect, I shouldn't have lied about Sunny in the first place. After I lied to you about him, you and I became close friends. I felt there was no need to tell you something we had already talked about and closed. I feared losing your trust and you, if I told you the truth. I had never imagined such excavation of my past would happen," she was out of breath.

"Believable story. By the way, how did you come to know about Myra's accident and her subsequent death? Nobody knew about it until the next evening, not even my parents. I also hadn't posted anything on social media. The newspapers also published it as a corner news piece a day later. But your calls started coming from the next morning itself, followed by your message mentioning you heard about her demise. Who told you?" I used my ace in the hole to play a winning hand.

Sensing she was at a complete loss of words, I said, "An *out-of-syllabus* question that you didn't prepare for?"

"Ah...um...," her eyeballs oscillated from one side to another, searching for an answer.

"Concocting a new story, Shalini?" my exasperation was shooting through the roof.

"Shruti, your cousin who was my classmate at school, told me," she tried her luck, but to no avail.

Shruti was close to me, but she was unaware of Myra's death until a few days later, when my parents had informed her.

"Again a lie! *Sach bol, sach bol, sach bol, haraamzadi*! I held her head between my hands and kept banging it on the bed till she said something that shook my core.

"I didn't want to kill her."

"What? What did you just say?" I was completely flabbergasted.

"Nothing," she was bawling.

"Say it!" I shook her head.

"Promise me, you will let me go if I tell you the truth," she pleaded.

"I promise," I gave her my commitment.

"What if you go back on your words?"

"You don't have a choice."

"It was an accident! I was not in my senses and I rammed into her," she confessed.

"Yyyou...were driving that car?" the shock dampened my voice and froze my brain for a few seconds.

"I am sorry, Abby."

"You killed Myra?" my voice quivered.

"Whyyyy?" I roared at her face and burst into tears.

"My intention was not to kill her. The initial plan was something else," she was trembling with fear.

I was almost knocked out with disbelief. I somehow managed to muster just enough strength to roll over and lie beside her with a blank stare at the ceiling, almost paralyzed as tears made their way from my eyes to the ears. All I could do was intermittently gulp the saliva down my dry throat as a knife seemed to cut endlessly through my heart, causing unbearable pain.

"What plan? I want to know everything," I asked getting back on top of her, even as the tornado of shock refused to abate.

"Mahesh and I had lost contact with each other after he had disappeared on me. When my marital troubles pushed me to the wall, I had posted a cryptic post on Facebook. I received a call from an unknown number that very day. It was Mahesh. I guess he was stalking me on Facebook."

"How did he get your number?" I controlled the urge to smash her face to death.

"I don't know. He must have sourced it from one of my batchmates or friends. He wanted to get back with me, but I was clear I didn't want to. He started pestering me with his calls and even showed up at my office a couple of times."

"How did Myra come into the picture?" I was getting impatient to know the truth.

"The time when Myra had caught you chatting with me late at night and misunderstood it to be our extramarital affair, she had messaged me on Facebook."

"Don't tell me things I already know."

"You know only a part of it. Her messages were very obnoxious and derogatory. I had explained and apologized to her, despite not being at fault. But she continued her rant and insulted me left, right and centre. She said I had dumped you when you needed me the most and that there was no need to be in touch with you when she was there for you. She called me a prostitute who was trying to break her home. She asked me if Sia was Prashant's child or if she was one of my clients'. I asked her to stop, but she was in no mood to relent. She said she would share my phone number with her rich friends who would pay enough to hire me as an escort. I just couldn't take it. She said she would inform Prashant, my parents, my friends and my relatives in my Facebook friend list, that I was having an illicit relationship with you. She had angered me to the hilt.

"I wanted to vent out, but I had nobody I could talk to about it and I couldn't sleep the whole night. To avenge myself for the sake of my self-respect, I decided I would blast her in person and show her, her rightful place. I left for Mumbai the next morning.

"On my way to Mumbai, we had interacted briefly when I told you that Myra had sent offensive messages to me the previous night, though I didn't tell you the exact content of those messages. You got pissed with Myra and decided to pick up your novel, instead of accompanying her to the sonography clinic. You didn't chat beyond that and said you will ping later.

"Moments later, Mahesh called me generally and asked where I was. When I told him I had just entered Mumbai, he requested to meet. I declined his offer in anger. Noticing my hyper state, he understood something was wrong and asked me about it. I said it was a long story and I would tell him when we met in person. He started insisting to meet and I gave in to his request.

"Mahesh intercepted my cab near Powai and picked me up in his Fortuner. I told him what all Myra had messaged. It irked him too. Since I knew Myra would take an auto-rickshaw to the clinic because she didn't know how to drive and preferred an auto-rickshaw to a cab, as per you, I decided to accost her right outside your society's main gate. While Mahesh and I were waiting for her at some distance from your main gate, Mahesh suggested not to engage with a bitch like her as she might retaliate, turning everyone around against me because she was pregnant. He proposed an idea to scare the daylights out of her, with his car. I got carried away with the idea as it seemed like a befitting lesson for her, and took over the wheels.

"As soon as I saw her come out of the main gate, I accelerated towards her to scare the shit out of her as a warning to never dare to engage with me in the manner she had done the previous night. I was so furious, I could see nothing else but Myra, and failed to notice little Rey on her other side. You had told me he would be at your neighbour's place and Myra would be going alone. So, I didn't even plan for such a case. When I saw Myra's face, her previous night's words started reverberating in my ears and fogged my mind to overpower my sanity. I don't know what got into me. In a fit of rage, as if possessed by evil, I rammed into her instead of evading her by a whisker. Once I hit her, I realized Rey was with her and I had hit him too. I panicked and decided to drive away, and in the process, ran over Myra," Shalini told me everything in one go.

"You killed Myra for such a trivial reason? While I understand she had said nasty things that she shouldn't have, you could have retorted with equally repugnant stuff on chat itself or on call. It didn't warrant her death. You knew she was pregnant," emotions were trying to choke me to death.

"I know I acted impulsively. Everything happened too fast for me to think things through with a sane and calm mind. Even then, the initial plan was never to kill her, Abby. I loved you; how could I intend to injure her gravely, knowing it could hurt or even kill your baby? I agree I didn't care a bit about Myra, but your unborn child was a part of you and I would never intend to hurt any part of you in any way. The car was supposed to scare her and at the most, brush against her. It was not supposed to run over her. It all happened because my anger and then my panic got the better of me," she said as I looked up at the ceiling and gasped for air to ease my breathlessness.

"Poor Rey, he loves you like his own mother, unaware of what you did to his mother and him," I was furious.

"Do you think I would ever hurt Rey? If you had notified me about his presence, I would have aborted my plan. I consider him my son as much as I consider Sia my daughter," she was sobbing.

"Oh! Save me your crap, Shalini. Do you know he was battling for his life in the ICU alongside Myra because of your impulsiveness and stupidity? The boy lost his mother because of you. So, don't talk about being a mother to him," I was fuming with anger.

"Why did Mahesh shield you for so long? He could have said the truth and turned you in. It would have saved him and his politician brother a lot of stress due to your wrong-doing," I moved on with my next question after a pause.

"Seeing me lose myself after the accident, he tried to calm me down saying he would handle things, but I was still scared. What if I got convicted in the end? So, I requested him to somehow keep me out of it completely and take the blame on himself if he has to."

"And he agreed? What a fool you made out of him?"

"Initially, he was hesitant but when I insisted, he gave me his words. He received a lot of backlash and stress due to the accident, but he stood his ground because he really loved me and somewhere in his heart, there was this guilt of ghosting me earlier."

"Was it just love and the guilt that made him commit or there was some *incentive* added from your side?"

"I promised to marry him," she said in a low tone.

"You have a habit of using and screwing people who love you, don't you? Lucky Prashant, he escaped."

"I had no alternative."

"Yeah, yeah, of course. You never do," I was agonized.

"What happened to your promise to marry him?" I continued.

"It was a meaningless promise that I had made during my emotional outburst to get my objectives sorted. I had no intention, whatsoever, of honouring my commitment to him. I told him we could get married only after my divorce came through, because in any case, I had to file for my divorce. It was convincing enough for him to postpone the talks of our marriage while I was just biding my time.

"When the divorce happened, you and I had a moment when we met at Patna. The spark of my feelings for you burst into flames. I started seeing a future with you. On the other hand, Mahesh started pressurizing me for marriage. In a bid to postpone the marriage talks yet again, I told him we could get married after Myra's case closed for good. Closure of the case would have also relieved me of the apprehensions of getting implicated in it. The safest way out of the case for me was its closure through your withdrawal of it. Since the case was going on endlessly, I convinced him to allow me some time to get closer to you and cajole you into withdrawing the case."

"Why didn't you tell him you didn't want to be with him anymore?" I asked her.

"If I had told him that upfront, why would he protect me? He would have easily got me implicated and set himself free. I needed him until the case was on. I had decided that once the legal sword hanging over my head would be gone, I would think of a way to get him off me.

"Mahesh had actually given me a teaser of the repercussions I would have to face if I backed off from my commitment to marry him. When you were not ready to withdraw the case despite my continued efforts, I kept asking him for more time and that made him suspicious about our blooming relationship. He got irritated and threatened he would incriminate me in Myra's case. I didn't attach too much weight to it, but he acted on his words and turned the case around, in which you and I were alleged to have plotted Myra's murder.

"I kept trying to convince you to withdraw the case, but you weren't ready at all. Even as time moved on, he continued harassing me with his pestering calls that did not seem to cease and I was under a perpetual undercurrent of stress that you asked me multiple times about, but I couldn't tell you.

"Then, the case started to see light at the end of the tunnel because of which I was really tensed. The case going on the right track might have led to my incrimination. After all, how long would Mahesh keep me out of it, especially when he had started doubting my feelings for him? Elections were around the corner and Mahesh's brother was making his life hell because his political career was getting affected due to it. When Mahesh discussed his concerns with me, I warned him that if I got implicated, he would be charged with felony too, because of his involvement in the murder and that would rub his brother and his political aspirations the wrong way. So, he had to play along. The only solution to save both of our asses was you letting go of the case. Our desperation to get off the hook and your bullheadedness of not withdrawing the case left me with no option but to plan your abduction."

"You were the mastermind behind my kidnapping? Why am I not surprised?"

It was inarguably the longest night of my life, full of staggering unfolding of events I was completely oblivious to.

"Come to think of it, it was also for your good, Abby. It freed you too, making your life easier and happier," she tried to tone me down.

"Don't justify your misdeeds. At what point of time did you plan my kidnapping?"

"Remember when I had come to Mumbai in August last year without informing you? You had got angry and I had to take a U-turn on my way to Pune to come to you. I had come to meet Mahesh and finalize the plan of your abduction. Not sure if you had noticed that time, I was completely zapped and messy. That son of a bitch had tried to force himself on me.

"About the need for abduction, I knew you inside-out and the only way to coerce you into withdrawing the case was to inject your mind with a thought of your loved ones suffering and getting harmed. You would do anything to protect them. The threat calls from unknown callers had proved futile in derailing you. So, as part of the plan, I asked him to abduct you and browbeat you into withdrawing the case by threatening you with devastating consequences that Rey and your loved ones might have to face. The plan worked and you withdrew the case.

"There was some respite for me, but when I kept postponing the talks of Mahesh and my marriage for over a month, his mistrust on me started crystallizing into confirmation and he started blackmailing me that he would spill the beans to you about Myra's murder if I didn't marry him. I somehow procrastinated it for a few months, but in January 2020, I decided enough was enough and it was time to solve the issue permanently because he was not going to relent. There were only two ways to get out of it – one, marrying him and two, conniving with you to kill him. I chose the latter because no matter how much he loved me, I loved you and wanted to live in peace with you. You know the story after that."

"How did you manage to keep him from executing his threats and keep his incessant demands to marry you at bay for those few months after I withdrew the case?"

"While you were busy with your job-hunt followed by your office projects at Mentor from September 2019 to January 2020, I was busy satiating his fantasies."

"Holy fuck! *Ab mujhe AIDS ka bhi test karana padega?*" I shouted at her.

"No, he used protection."

"Zip up, shameless! What happened after January?"

"In February too, I had to continue the same story with him to make him feel loved, but thankfully, lockdown saved me from March onwards. After that, everything with him was only virtual."

"Before you decided to go for my Plan B, how were you planning to shake him off you? Having sex with him was always going to be a temporary solution."

"I had thought he would get bored of me after getting physical with me multiple times, but he was as unswerving as a mule and he stuck to his demand to marry me."

"Right, those who love you deeply become mules. I suppose I was one too. Anyway, what Mahesh claimed about Myra's character, was there any truth to it?" I asked her.

"No, I knew how your mind operated when angry and I simply used it to my advantage. I have experienced it first-hand when I broke up with you. I also knew that once the case closed, you would do something beyond the scope of law to punish Mahesh because of your innate vindictiveness. I didn't want that because I wanted you to move on with me. So, I planted the seed of Myra's betrayal in your mind through Mahesh and then corroborated it with forged evidence. Tarnishing Myra's character and proving that she had betrayed you served dual purpose. One, your love for her decamped your heart to make way for mine. Two, you felt cheated and short-changed, and stopped fighting for her in anger. It helped my cause, you shunned your Plan B too with immediate effect. Myra was innocent, Abby and her character was unimpeachable," Shalini admitted the truth.

My interrogation was like sending a cat among the pigeons as it sent the events of my life fluttering in front of my eyes in an unimaginable light. I had no idea facing the ugly truth behind the disaster in my life would be so mind-numbing and shattering. The moment of epiphany emasculated me. My heart ached for judging Myra. I knew she had an unquestionable character, but one stone of doubt thrown in my lake of trust by an outsider and I magnified its splash to a tsunami. This, however, was not that big a revelation than Shalini being behind Myra's death for a reason as trifling as it was. Somewhere, I was responsible for Myra's death. I shouldn't have let a double-dealing Shalini back into my life.

Though I had got into all the details of Shalini's step-by-step plan to feed my curiosity and to not err in my judgement that would follow, the bottom line was that she had killed Myra and Mahesh was her accomplice.

The volcano of Myra's memories and my dormant love for her erupted in my mind. Long-forgotten events and sensations resurfaced from the depths of my past, making me feel the unliftable burden of Myra's love. It was as if the guilt in my heart had blown up several balloons inside, making my chest pain with the stiffness and breathlessness it induced. It was time to burst some of them.

CHAPTER 21

Location: Mumbai
Time: June 2020

"I told you everything, Abby. I kept my promise, it is time for you to keep yours. Let me go," she pleaded.

"Shove that promise up your ass. Not keeping promises is the order of the day, Shalini," I was eager to execute my judgement.

"What do you mean?" she still believed the *naïve* Abby would keep his words.

"Since the time you made a comeback to my life, I have been nothing but a remote-controlled missile with its controller in your hands. You wiped off Myra from my life and scripted my descent into the rabbit hole. You were the reason for my misery when we first dated years ago and you have been the reason for my affliction ever since you returned to my life. What you did was very, very wrong and utterly unpardonable. You shouldn't have done it. I loved you so much, Shalini but... Now, I will have to do something very bad to you."

"No apology or act of penitence is enough to atone for my sins, but nothing can doubt my love for you. Please don't kill me for the heck of it," she had an idea of what might befall her.

"I will take that into consideration," I reassured her.

"My failed execution of the plan to teach Myra a lesson was just destiny's way to execute its own plan of her death. If it had not happened through me, it would have happened through somebody else. You never realized, you were in an abusive relationship. Think about it, she didn't respect you the way I do, she didn't love you the way I do, she never craved for you the way I do. She never valued you, Abby," she tried to claw back by pricking my non-existent hatred for Myra.

"Whatever moments of discord happened between Myra and I were part and parcel of any couple's married life. She had her own nature of being vocal about issues while I had mine of being silent and that was our personal equation which worked beautifully for us. You think she didn't value me? Did you value me? Whatever she was, she was to my face. She didn't live two lives like you did. She was never pretentious like you were. She never manipulated me like you did. She was with me in my toughest of times and that speaks tons about her love which you have the audacity to question," I wasn't ready to forgive her.

"I am pregnant with your child, Abby," she wouldn't give up trying.

"Perfect na? Myra was also pregnant. The last time we made love was months ago and I had used precaution. I didn't know my tongue had the virility to impregnate you. I will be mindful of this superpower in my next relationship," I mocked her.

Stuffing the cloth back into her mouth, I ambled to the living room to return with the blindfold and a glass of vodka.

As soon as she saw what I was holding, she started shaking her head desperately with a continuous grunt.

"Don't move, you will hurt yourself," I blindfolded her.

"I am going to remove the cloth from your mouth. If you try to shout, I will chop your tongue off with this knife," I ran the edge of the knife on her face.

"Think about Sia who you consider as your daughter. She will never be able to see me. She will lose her mother. Have a heart, Abby," she played the emotional card.

"Do you think Rey will ever be able to see his mother? He lost his mother too. I didn't even get a chance to say goodbye to the love of my life. Did you have a heart?"

"Don't kill me, Abby. I will confess my crime in front of the police. You can record a video of my confession right now. I am willing to accept whatever punishment law decides for me," she was an incorrigible fighter who would fight until her last breath.

"I don't believe in the law of the land anymore. I believe in my *Law of Revenge*. So, it has to be a life for a life, sweetheart," I was ready for the final shot.

"But my intention was not to kill her. And I love you, Abby. Doesn't your law demand protecting your love?"

"The love for Myra comes before yours. However, I will consider your feelings and give you a painless death," I pinched her nose to close it, forcing her mouth to open to gasp for air.

"Rest in peace baby," possessed by a demon who was restless to unleash himself on her, I downed the vodka spiked with 10 mg of Rohypnol into her mouth and stuffed it back with the cloth.

She coughed, but the lethal shot was already down her throat. Hearing her relentless, heart-wrenching sobs pained my heart and threatened to haunt me for the rest of my life. The moments of happiness I shared with her started flitting in front of my eyes, inundating them with tears. Her sparkling eyes, her succulent lips, her euphonious voice, her soft and caring touch, the natural fragrance of her body, everything started conspiring and screwing with my mind to overturn the punishment I had just meted out to her for her misdeeds, but I had to embrace the role that the universe had laid out for me.

"People say first love is always special. You know why? It is because it is pure, which is why it never dies, no matter how hard one tries. I will always love you for all the happy moments you gifted me with. I so wish you had not killed my Myra; I would have forgiven you for everything else. I am sorry! I promise if Prashant doesn't take up Sia's responsibility, I will. Both Sia and Rey will never get to know the evil side of you. Regardless of what comes out in the news in the days that follow, I will make sure both of them always remember you as an ideal mother and have nothing but unadulterated love for you. Your role in this world is over, my love. May you find peace in another!" I said as she kept whimpering in the background.

As minutes passed, her sobs became gentler and gentler before fading into the silence of the room. Within the next half an hour, the air in the room completely engulfed her feeble breaths while my tear-laden eyes watched from the sidelines. My Shalini was no more!

Mahesh had not murdered Myra, but he had played a part in it. In my court of justice, he was an accomplice who was also guilty of obstruction of justice by withholding information to shield Shalini. So, I would not kill him as per my initial plan, but a punishment commensurate with his involvement in the crime had to be awarded and it didn't take me long to think about it.

It was 2.00 a.m. and my race against time had intensified. I had to keep my emotions aside and set up the crime scene in accordance with the new story I wanted the world to believe before rigor mortis kicked in and stiffened Shalini's body.

I carried Mahesh on my shoulder to the same bed where Shalini laid lifeless and removed his clothes. With his mouth open, he was still breathing. He had no idea what series of events he had passively witnessed. 4 mg of the drug was not actually a fatal overdose for a guy like him, but would keep him out for a day. I decided not to overdose him further because I wanted him to live and suffer.

I unshackled Shalini to undress her while constantly flicking my eyes over to Mahesh to check on him; haste and a bit of nervousness warring my expression. I removed the cloth stuffed in her mouth and tossed it beside her on the bed.

All the primary items that were part of the plot – handcuffs, ropes, blindfold, cloth, Rohypnol sachets, glasses, Red Bull can, butcher knife, Shalini's clothes, etc., I clutched them one by one, using Mahesh's hands, so as to put his fingerprints on them.

I turned the stinky giant to his side and touched Shalini's body all over with his hands, especially the private ones, and repeated the process with Shalini's hands on his body. I extracted saliva from Mahesh's open mouth using cotton buds and applied it on various parts of Shalini's body. I put his hands at the two places he would have held her body from if he had carried her.

The next round had me transferring plucked hair from strategic locations on either body to the other, followed by digging Shalini's nails deep into Mahesh's skin to scrape some of his DNA. For the final touch, I rolled Mahesh's body over Shalini's and dug his teeth into her cheek.

I lifted Shalini's delicate body that had become heavier, and put it on the washroom floor under the turned off shower. I carried Mahesh too, to the washroom. Holding him in sitting position facing Shalini, I let him fall freely on the floor sideways. I put my butcher knife in his hand and placed a few garbage bags (from his kitchen) beside him after putting his fingerprints on them.

I spent an hour more to look for any blunder that I might have made, so that I could make amends. I wanted to be absolutely certain that the cops formed the hypothesis I wanted them to form and when they rummaged through the house looking for proofs to corroborate their initial theory, they would find every piece of evidence shouting at the top of its voice that it belonged to my story. I left the apartment and the society in my PPE suit at about 5 a.m., keeping my fingers crossed. No one bothered.

By afternoon, my horrendous crime would be all over the news channels and internet. From the storyline that the cops and the media would project, my fate would be more or less sealed – as a bestial convict (in the future) or a free, content and innocent man.

CHAPTER 22

Location: Mumbai
Time: June 2020

Article published on 12 June 2020 on a leading news portal:

Kin of noted politician kills techie girlfriend with drug overdose

Mumbai: *Mahesh Prajapati, brother of noted politician, Somesh Prajapati purportedly murdered his alleged techie girlfriend with a drug overdose and had plans of dismembering her body, but he seemed to have passed out before he could do so. The thirty-six-year-old deceased woman, identified as Shalini, was employed with a reputed multi-national software company in Pune and had accompanied Mahesh last night to his apartment in an upscale locality in Lokhandwala, Andheri (West), as per eyewitnesses. Her identity was confirmed through her company ID that she was carrying in her handbag.*

"Saheb asked me to stay over at the driver's place yesterday. He said he was expecting some guest and I was not needed. When I reported to work at around 11 a.m. today as per his instructions, he did not open the door. He was not picking up my

calls either. So, I opened the door with my spare key. I saw Saheb and a woman lying motionless in the bathroom. I immediately called the police," Mahesh's twenty-four-hour domestic help, Deva said.

The police found Mahesh and Shalini in the bathroom of his apartment under mysterious circumstances. Both of them were rushed to the hospital. While Shalini was pronounced dead on arrival, Mahesh is being treated in the ICU. Cops suspect it to be a case of drug overdose.

"We have sent the woman's body for post-mortem and are waiting for Mahesh to regain consciousness so that we can record his statement. Prima facie, it looks like a classic drug overdose case, but we will investigate all angles. Our forensics team is collecting fingerprints and gathering other forensic evidence that will help us recreate the sequence of events. We will be in a better position to make an official statement once the preliminary reports are out by day after tomorrow," said Shivram Tripathi, Deputy Superintendent of Police (DSP), Mumbai.

Tens of similar news pieces spread across the internet and news channels by the evening of 12 June. The murder felt like my examination and the initial forensic report was my report card. Whether or not I would pass, I would only get to know a couple of days later when the cops would release an official statement. As a child, I used to tell myself before my report card day, "*Chill Abby, not a matter of life and death.*" But this time, it was actually a matter of life and death. With bated breath and fingers crossed, I waited for my result battling anxiety, panic and a perennial cold sweat.

Article published on 14 June 2020 in a leading daily:

A kinky encounter that went terribly wrong, confirms Mumbai Police on Mahesh Prajapati-Shalini case

Mumbai: *Mumbai Police seem to have cracked the Mahesh Prajapati – Shalini case in record time despite challenges posed due to surge in Covid cases. In an official statement released by Mumbai Police, DSP Shivram Tripathi said, "Call and chat records of Mahesh and Shalini reveal they had known each other for a long time and were in a relationship. Mahesh's chats on Shalini's phone were deleted, however, we recovered them from Mahesh's phone. There was no third person involved and it was a planned kinky sex night that went terribly wrong. A drug named Rohypnol (commonly known as the date-rape drug) was found in the apartment as well as in the bodies of Shalini and Mahesh who purportedly used it to experience a high during their intimate encounter.*

"As per the preliminary forensics report, Shalini was apparently handcuffed to the bed and blindfolded by a drugged Mahesh, and then forcibly given an extra dose of the drug to enhance his experience. What started as a consensual encounter turned into a sexual assault but before penetrative sex could happen, Shalini died due to the overdose. In panic, Mahesh carried her body to the washroom to chop it into pieces and later dispose it off. Due to the overdose of the drug, he passed out himself while attempting to dismember her body, with a butcher knife in his hand and garbage bags beside him.

"Recovery of evidence like Mahesh's fingerprints on Shalini's body, her clothes, knife, handcuffs, ropes, blindfold, etc., along with DNA traces on each other's body and the state in which the bodies were found in the washroom, as well as assault indicators like Mahesh's bite mark on Shalini's face, his DNA in the skin

cells found under her nails, tears on her face and the blindfold, bruises on her wrists and ankles, reinforce our theory. We have also scanned the CCTV footage of Mahesh's home and saw him turning off the CCTV cameras himself at around 8 p.m. It is an open and shut case. Though Mahesh claims he does not remember anything and is innocent, he has been arrested and will be charged with culpable homicide not amounting to murder, and rape under relevant sections of the IPC."

Shalini was a divorced mother of a seven-year-old girl and lived with her parents in Pune. Calls and messages to her parents did not elicit a response.

Mahesh's brother and noted politician, Somesh Prajapati whose political career has already taken severe blows due to the nefarious activities of his brother, isn't shocked. "This was expected and it was only a matter of time when this would happen. We were brothers, however, I was never a part of his life and we weren't in touch of late. He probably deserves his fate. Please keep me out of this. My life has always been dedicated to the people of Maharashtra and my only focus in life is to uplift their lives. If they have faced any inconvenience because of me, I apologize to them," he said, distancing himself from the controversy surrounding his brother's life.

My results were out and I had not just qualified my examination, I had topped it! I had delivered the coup de grace with aplomb and enacted a future bestseller in real-life. An unfortunate and mysterious demise of one of the most loved, talented, sincere and hardworking Bollywood actors on 14 June, and alarming Covid-19 fatalities in the country stole the limelight from a relatively insignificant Mahesh-Shalini case. I believe, the political pressure from a selfish Somesh to brush things under